CW01457115

A Boy, a Dog and the Great War

Daniel Carlson

Copyright© 2025Daniel Carlson

This book is a work of fiction based upon factual and historical events.

All rights reserved. No part of this book may be reproduced in any form or by any electronic or mechanical means, including information storage and retrieval systems, without permission in writing from the author, except by reviewers, who may quote brief passages in a review.

Cover by Carl Goodall

All rights reserved.

Chapter 1

Winter 1917

Bertie Lanyon could not recall how many times he'd been sitting in the grass on the cliff top, staring out into nothingness. Ritually and almost every day, as soon as he could, he'd sped from his small terraced cottage to squat with his knees tucked up to his chest and his arms wrapped around them to glare out in the direction of France.

He did not know what he hoped to see, and he dare not allow his imagination to run wild, but he knew what to expect. By day endless miles of bluey grey, occasionally dotted by tiny fishing boats that bobbed in the far distance and disappearing from sight where the sky merged with the sea. Night time was much worse, offering nothing, but pitch, yet it didn't prevent him from scrutinizing the darkness. Once in a while there'd be a moon shimmering on the black surface and from time to time there'd be the twinkling of a red or green light from the unfortunate hookers and reelers who applied their trade in the midst of darkness, but out there amongst undulating swells there were no battleships, nor the invasion fleet everyone once feared.

Unlike the balmy summer nights, where he'd welcomed the breeze to cool his sundried skin, tonight's rafts of rain and coldness chilled his spine and numbed his face. He clapped his hands to generate warmth, and he blew warm breath down through the neck of his jumper onto his chest. Considering a retreat to the tall wooden structure twenty yards behind him, he patted his sides, rubbed his back, and swivelled his neck.

He could hear the banter and the laughter, for those inside it was the first time in many years, but he wasn't in the mood to join in the fun, and he decided against it, besides this was his spot where he'd crouched, scanned the coast and reminisced for the last three years and he wasn't going to allow just a cold sea breeze and the threat of a storm to uproot him. If the brave lads on the front lines could endure the bitterest of weather whilst the earth around them shook from continual bombardments, then he could withstand a mere tempestuous gust. However, the shivers did disturb his thoughts and with the passing of the angry clouds above he wondered, 'How did the long hot days and tranquil nights pass so quickly from one season to the next?' Maybe it was the almighty's doing. Had he accepted the prayers of the many thousands who daily willed the hours to pass quickly because their loved ones were suffering in the trenches? Or had the seasons just rolled almost unnoticed from one into another by only Bertie and his friends who had frolicked away their days playfully on the peaceful and beautiful cliff tops.

Within the groans of the swirling gusts which chilled his back, he was sure he could hear Millie calling out warnings.

"Don't slip on that rock."

She was the caring one with an intrinsic kindness, always on the lookout for danger and worrying about the wellbeing of others. Her high-pitched cautions were as clear to Bertie as they were 4 years ago when he, Drake, Newt and Lily foraged amongst the rocks for treasures washed up by the sea.

"Don't stand on the seaweed." She repeated as Drake, the defiant and daring one, slipped and fell backwards with so much speed that his legs shot forwards and rose so uncontrollably high that he almost kicked himself in the face. That was Drake, always doing the opposite of what 'mothering' Millie told him, endangering himself to show off in front of her, and when he did hurt himself to shock and impress her he would always pull away the scabs on his knees and elbows.

Being older and wiser to life's ways now, Bertie knew that was Drake's way of flirting with Millie, and Millie being just eleven and innocent of any romantic notions, fumed, blustered and cussed as she lost her temper to his continual showy recklessness.

He allowed himself half of a smile. He could never recall a time when he had been without the gang. They'd always been around one another, together as a gang. He couldn't really imagine being without them, but then again, he knew the hard way that everything eventually comes to an end.

Gradually Bertie's smile faded, and his memories receded. He once more stared out into the nothingness, cloud covered moon and no stars, just sheer pitch with an occasional flash of lightening in the distance, but he knew the sea was there below him, just as it always was, pounding against the rocks just as it did when his father was lost to the black waters just a few years earlier, and before the start of the mass deaths, and before the villages were accustomed to the deaths of their young. A tear blurred greyness and then blinded, he wiped his eyes clear with his knuckles. He sighed, drew a breath and held it to compose himself.

5

He was used to it now. Controlling the returning melancholy had now become as natural to him as sleeping and waking. Even when he couldn't occupy his thoughts with a pleasant distraction, he'd finally adapted to the ever wondering thoughts of where his father's body was. Every night for years, it had been the same nauseating questioning. *'Did he die inside the boat?' 'Is he still trapped inside?' 'Was his body bashed against the rocks?' 'Or did he simply drown to be eaten by the fish?'* He knew he'd never know, he understand that, but it didn't prevent the reoccurring nightmares, the endless searching in his dreams and the inevitable sadness. He shouldn't have gone out that night. He knew it, they all knew it, but what choice did he have?

There'd been no work in South Cliff since the tin mine closed nine years ago, leading to the spread of poverty that ravaged through the local industries. Most folks in South Cliff, and the surrounding villages were afforded enough charity from their relatives to abandoned their homes and forge a livelihood elsewhere, but for those who were not so fortunate, and had nowhere else to go, their desperation resulted in risky ventures of which they were not accustomed to.

For the few in South Cliff who had no choice, but to stay in their now worthless homes, some found seasonal work in the fields, two of the men worked away from home only returning once every couple of months, and Bertie's father, Bert and his close friend were offered employment by Taddy Dimmock, the last remaining fisherman to work out of the timeworn harbour in South Cliff. Although Taddy worked the small boat from dawn until dusk, he was prepared to rent out the boat for the evening shift to anyone willing to pay him 25 percent of their profits.

Bert and his friend had little experience of being on the seas, as with most in the coastal village he'd been on the waters with his own father when the seas were bountiful, but that was many years ago when they still called themselves Victorians.

They were reckless and shouldn't have gone out that night. Both men knew it, all the family knew it and everyone in the village knew it, yet no one spoke about the onset of the nearing storm. The late afternoon had delivered dense low clouds and an eerie dullness which muffled all sound, hindered vision and foretold of the bad weather to come.

His Ma had been soulless ever since. Blamed herself for pressuring him to work and for not stopping him from going out when the waves began to roll in ever higher.

Now and from that moment in the unforgiving night, she'd only been able to unburden her grief by relying upon copious doses of Mrs Hecklaw's home made restorative remedy. The plain black bottle of her kindly neighbour's soothing potion and sleeping tonic was readily available at her request and never too far from her grip.

There'd been no frivolity since thenceforth. She lost any joyous spirit that had been spared from the poverty, and she had become soulless and void of emotion. Surviving in an empty shell of her previous being, she cooked, cleaned and begged desperately for work.

Another wet bluster shuddered him, it was not the cool breeze he welcomed in the summer, but one which shivered his every bone.

Again, he wrapped his arms around his sides and patted his body to warm himself, and then he caught another glimpse of what was lurking behind him.

Barely visible in the gloom, standing tall just twenty strides from the cliff top was the wooden clad structure that only yesterday filled his heart with pride. He swivelled to glance at the crude creation which omitted hints of light, singing and laughter from it's ill-fitting planks.

It didn't mean anything to him now. The entertainment and the hope of filling the hearts of the locals with joy had lost it's appeal, for crumpled in his hand was the letter from the post boy which his Ma had not been brave enough to open.

The muffled noise of the frivolity, the echoes of laugher and the sound of the music which breeched the gaps in the planks could do nothing to ease his pain. He straightened his back and ambled towards the strong wind which blew in from the sea, only stopping when he saw below him the bellowing whiteness of the waves crashing into the rocks below.

Briefly, he turned his back to the sea and listened to the howling gusts behind him swirl across the wild grass to creak and clatter, and raise and drop the inelegant wooden boards of his theatre.

'I've done it.' He thought without absorbing the pride which was rightfully his. *'My idea.'*

He denied himself the smile of satisfaction and shook his head. Then arching his back to reduce the resistance of the increasing gusts, he turned away from the building and took another step closer to the cliff top.

Another icy blast quivered him and pimpled his skin, or was it trepidation as he began to recall the happenings of four years ago.

Closing his eyes, he took a deep breath of the crisp winter air and positioned himself at the edge of the cliff.

He could feel the hollowness under the spongy grass beneath his feet. He swayed and stared into the grumbling abyss below as the strong wind battered against him, but then as it eased he straightened himself once more and, drawing in a lung filling breath, he finally roused enough courage to open the letter.

Chapter 2

"Ma! Come quick! Bertie, come here now! The both you."

Bertie was resting on his bed when James burst open the kitchen door with excitable fervency to begin repeatedly hollering out with ear bursting urgency.

"Ma! Bertie. Where are you?"

He'd not been home long after working in Old Man Corney's field. He was exhausted, hungry, and his neck was sore from the scorching sun. All he wanted to do was rest up a while, with his best friend Finn curled up by his side, and wait for his Ma to cook supper.

As usual, he was looking forward to going down into Horseshoe Cove with his four pals to scavenge amongst the sea battered rocks for washed up treasure as they did every night in the summer.

"Come on. Where are you?" James urged.

'Bugger' He'd be in trouble again if Finn barked or bounded down the bare wooden stairs to greet his older brother.

"Shush Finn," he whispered, wrapping his fingers around the retriever's ginger snout. "Easy boy." He urged as he scooped up the dog in his arms, it's tail flapping across his face with both excitement and bewilderment. "Mustn't let Ma hear you up here, boy."

He heard James open the door to the hallway. "Ma! Bertie!"

"I'm coming," he shouted back as he wrestled to hold Finn close to his chest.

"What do you want?" he asked, somewhat relieved by the lack of a response from his Ma confirming she was not in the house.

"Just get down here now."

"Why?" He delayed, waiting for James to return to the kitchen.

"Just do as I say."

He waited until he heard James's cumbersome footsteps thump back into the kitchen.

"Where's Ma?"

Bertie did not answer. He couldn't, he needed all his breath to haul his wriggling friend along the narrow passageway and down the stairs without hurting him.

"I'm here."

He heard his Ma shout just as he safely knee'd open the kitchen door and lowered Finn's paddling feet to the floor.

"What in blazers is going on?" She asked, entering the house cradling an arm full of beets and carrots.

"Not now, boy." Between panting breaths, James gently forearmed away the bounding dog as he leaped towards him with out-stretching paws and a draft creating wagging tail. "Get down."

Unable to comprehend what exited his normally placid brother, Bertie only inched into the room and looked at him from the doorway.

"Come sit." James dragged out two chairs from under the table, and then turning, he took the handful of soiled roots from his mother. "Sit now." He tossed them into the tin bowl. "Quickly sit now."

"What?" She scowled.

"Sit."

Remaining static and confused, James used the flat of his palm to guide his Ma to her chair. "Come on! This is very important."

He frowned at Bertie and slanting his head he nodded in the direction of the empty chair indicating he wanted his brother not to waste any more time.

"What is so important? James, what's wrong?" she asked bewilderedly.

James arched forward and leant over the table with his knuckles pressed against the wood.

"It's war." He exclaimed with a nervous pitch.

"What is?" Bertie frowned.

"Germany has invaded Belgium." He said, inhaling slow breaths between each word.

"Germany?" The widow gasped and dropped her head into her hands. "Belgium but....."

"And now they've attacked France." James rushed.

"Mister Asquith has made a speech in the house."

"House?" Bertie swivelled his head away from his Ma's angered face to James.

"Parliament." James's eyes widened. "He has informed the country that he has given Germany an ultimatum."

"A what?" Bertie couldn't prevent himself from cutting in.

"Ultimatum." His brother's carefree ignorance broke James's patience, and he slammed his fist on to the table. "Do as I say, or there will be trouble."

"What? ....Sorry." Bertie's face flushed and his embarrassment caused him to look away.

"No." James corrected. "Do as I say or there will be trouble is kind of an ultimatum." James turned over his palms to express his frustration. "Now will you let me finish."

"Why has he done that?" She sighed, raised her hands to cover her face and squeezed her eyes tight to prevent tears from falling.

"Don't think he had any option." He pulled out the spare chair "It's very complicated," and sank into it's seat. "But when the Germans started their bullying, he, Mr Asquith .... our Prime Minister promised the rest of Europe that we'd protect them and that he wouldn't let the Huns invade any other countries."

"And?" Still ignorant to the significance, Bertie patted his thigh to capture Finn's attention.

"And.....and......... You bloody fool! It only means we are at sodding war!"

"James … language." His Ma groaned and raised her head out from her palms, her face suddenly pale.

"Sorry Ma. I couldn't help it."

"We're going to war?" Bertie had to repeat, his hands reaching under the table and stretching to find the brow of Finn. Suddenly, he felt the need to give his friend a comforting pat.

"That's right Bertie boy. We are at war!"

James seemed pleased it was he who delivered the shocking and terrifying news. He'd been in Trewin looking for work, seven miles north of South Cliff, when he saw a gathering that was locked in a fierce arm waving debate. Once he had digested the enormity of the reports, he sprinted the entire distance, leaping over stone walls and hedges, and racing through the shoulder high crops to ensure he was the first to deliver the news to the handful of villagers who remained in South Cliff.

"The King has already called up the reservists, and it looks like, from what I heard, is that many more are willing and ready to follow."

"I don't understand." Returning her blank gaze to the pattern of the grain on the table top their Ma shook her head. "Even if the Germans have behaved horrendously, what has it got to do with us?"

"Because the meddlesome Germans won't stop until they've conquered all of Europe to eventually make it their own Empire." He clamped his hand over his Ma's shaking palm to stop it from shaking the table top. "Be everyone master, including us."

She momentarily tilted her face towards him. He saw fear in her eyes, and although he squeezed her trembling hand, her entire body shuddered.

"I'm not learning German." Bertie shook his head and peaked under the table. "Are we Finn?" The dog wagged his tail and grunted.

"Then you'd be the one of the first to get your tongue cut out." James leaned across the table.

"Stop it! Stop it now." She pulled away her hand from under James's palm and scraped back the chair. "Both of you." She rose quickly and moved towards the window to stare blankly across the fields towards the English Channel. "Stop all this nonsense." She tried to distract herself by fumbling and brushing off dirt from the carrots.

"But it's true Ma. All of it."

"Enough James."

"It will be in all the newspapers tomorrow."

"Enough I said. I don't want to hear any more about it." The tin thudded as she threw down the carrots. "I don't want to hear anymore about the Germans or the war." Although the volume was low, her words carried force.

James slumped back against the chair spindles. "It's not going to go away."

Bertie held his breath, his hand feathering Finn's ear. "Then we shall read all about it tomorrow," she calmly announced. "But enough is enough for one night."

15

Chapter 3

The bland root stew was cooked and eaten in apprehensive silence that evening, and afterwards the hours hurried by with a mixture of excitable, but illogical speculation as Bertie and the gang sat in the long grass looking out at the restless waves expecting to see a bustle of flotillas. However, nothing out of the ordinary happened in South Cliff that evening nor over the next few weeks.

Bertie worked in Old Man Corney's field in the unusual glorious sun, and after supper he rendezvous every evening with his pals down in Horseshoe Cove to explore and rummage through the tidal treasures. Disappointingly, as normal nothing too exciting was discovered, just the regular wash ups of wood, broken bottles and rope, lots of rope.

At times, Bertie was not as eager to beach comb as Millie, Drake, Newt and Lily, and lapsing into a melancholic sullenness he'd slip away with Finn to sit and just stare from a distance for fear that one day amongst the seaweed and shells they might discover something of his fathers.

As was their routine when the eastern sky began to darken they would assemble their horde and hide it away in Quintal's Cave full well knowing, that whilst occasionally some villagers may take a gentle stroll down the cobbles to the old harbour on the other side of the bay, no one would dare to tread the treacherous snaking path which led the way through wild bushes to the high-backed and Pirate haunted rocky cove. Up to the cliff top was always their next destination, sometimes gathering around a small campfire to play with the amber glowing wood and eat the black, red and blue berries that Millie and Lily had picked with stoic reliability.

A Boy, a Dog and the Great War

Other nights they'd play hopscotch, skip and race each other until it was too dark to see, then exhausted, they'd lie back on the spongy grass talking about the imaginary visions they could see in the twinkling of the bright stars as below them fierce tides hissed and thundered against the rocks.

Finn was always there enjoying himself and joining in with their playful antics. He's sniff amongst the rock pools, dug in the sand, and contribute to their collections with his extrasensory perception of all things interesting, and when the playing was done, he'd cuddle in alongside them and roll in the grass, snuggling up from one to the other until he got a good rub and tickle.

All too fast, the darkness began to arrive earlier every night and their faces dampened with the approaching autumn low hanging mists. They lamented the passing of the long hot summer and for Millie, Lily, and Newt, the encroachment of the boring return to the classroom in Trewin seven miles away.

As expected Drake, who was more often silly than serious, teased, tormented and ridiculed the three youngsters for having to return to their studies whilst he, being the same age as Bertie twelve, was no longer was required to attend the classroom, and now with men enlisting in huge numbers, he boasted that he would soon find work with regular pay. Being gifted with an easy tongue, Bertie did not doubt his friends his confidence for one moment, but his gloating at the expense of others irked him and he cut short Drake's swagger by pointing out he was hoping to profit from the absence of someone's father, son or brother.

17

Drake was embarrassed at being berated in front of the girls and the hurling of fists was only prevented by Millie, who stepped in between the boys fighting stance to scream and plead with them to stop their senselessness. Finally, after lots of cursing, they turned away from each other, diverting their attentions to stoking the small flames of the campfire instead of each other.

Neither of the boys regretted their behaviour. Drake's bravado in front of Millie and his continually bullying of the others irritated Bertie, and Drake only lowered his fists first because Millie begged him to and he wanted to please her.

Neither of them listened to Newt's nervous prattle as he tried to distract them by announcing he had heard his Pa and his uncle talking about enlistment. He said his Pa had returned from Trewin with a warning that the government was introducing a selective service act meaning any fit man aged between 21 and 30 could be called up to the big fight. With tears welling, and leaning on Lily for support he said he'd heard his Pa say to his uncle he was not going to wait to be embarrassed by being drafted, and that he was going to volunteer when the recruitment officers next came to Trewin.

Aghast and engulfed with sympathy for Newt the girls asked him question after question which he could not answer, whilst both Bertie and Drake simply prodded the fire and sat in ponderous silence.

The gang's nightly routine continued in the usual way, with no mention of the quarrel. Although mainly oblivious to what was happening overseas, every night each one of them fervently relayed the war gossip they collected from the village hearsayers.

With most of the village boarded up including the grocery store, post office and the tavern, up-to-date news had become an eagerly sought, valuable asset and so the post boy who rode over from Trewin every Tuesday and Friday suddenly found himself so popular his return journey was delayed by over an hour. No one sensible could rely on the Friday night declarations which the men folk slurred. By the time they had made the cart journey home from there weekly visit to the Hound and Rabbit in Trewin, the ale they had consumed in large volumes made them almost incoherent, and by the time the sun arose the following morning they had mainly forgotten what news they had been told.

The trip to church, the first Sunday of the new month was no longer considered a wasted morning of drudgery. However, still mainly uninterested, the gang would mumble along to hymns whilst daydreaming of running wild in the fields or foraging for berries and bird's eggs amongst the trees instead of listening to the two-hour boring sermon, which they failed to understand. Yet, now the gathering had become an important social centre for meaningful and up-to-date briefings which grabbed everyone's ear, including the Vicars.

The few daily's which found their way on to the kitchen tables in South Cliff were often grubby, days old and well handled. The few men who had remained in the village worked long hours in the fields, so it was left to the women, when they needed provisions they couldn't grow or make themselves, to make the half day foot trek to the nearest store and return with the factual printed account. Once thoroughly read the paper would be passed over the fence from neighbour to neighbour and sometimes even back again.

If it hadn't been for the war, and his Ma's despondency, the remaining days of that magnificent summer had almost seemed too perfect for Bertie. Almost every day after work he'd swim in the sea, and he'd join up with the gang to ritually collect the treasures washed up in the rocks, and then as their routine dictated, they'd race along the cliff tops and play football until darkness hailed full time.

In early September, to mark the return to school, the townsfolk of Trewin organised their annual summer fete, and alongside the craft stalls, Duggett's fair would come into town to take over the whole green by erecting coconut shies, shooting galleries, hoop la's and merry-go rounds.

As the previous year, Bertie and Drake eagerly led the way to Trewin by climbing over stone walls, carefully navigating through sheep cropped turf and cornfields, and by treacherously feeling their way through thorn hedges, they trimmed the journey time by over an hour.

Although they had little money to spend, amongst the butterflies and the flower scented warm air they skipped and ran with eager merriment until finally they could feast their eyes, and tease their nostrils upon the enticements baited by Duggett's lure.

Drake was full of his usual swagger, repeatedly showing off and tripping Newt, whose clumsy feet didn't need any further hindrance. He'd been wearing his father's old work boots and already that day there had been too many occasions to recall when Newt had raised his leg and left an empty boot in the grass.

After a few miles he was fed up with being ridiculed and he wanted to give up and go home, but Bertie, being a full head taller, insisted that he swap footwear with him for the day and continue on to Trewin. Finally, even with Drake's resentful irritation, they were soon back on their way.

Taking Bertie by the hand, his kind behaviour gladdened Millie, and squeezing it tight, she made him promise to sit with her on the carousel. The unexpected invite at first reddened his face, but accepting without hesitation, adapting his pace to match her steps, and walking with beaming smile he had unintentionally infuriated Drake further, and now fearing the lack of attention Drake took out his frustration by teasing both Millie and Lily by throwing insects in their hair and berries against their floral dresses.

Beyond the village green, not too far away from the noise and the salivating smells of the fete, erected strategically outside the Hound and Rabbit, was a green draped stall they'd never seen before.

A line of chattering men had formed, and within minutes it become so long that it blocked out the entrance into the fruit and vegetable shop and it had stretched the length of the High Street beyond the butchers and round the corner.

So jovial was their spirits that the gang could hear their patriotic optimism and claim the Hun would soon turn and run. Between lungful's of cigarette smoke and bellows of grey smoke, it was obvious to all, the boastful men were united in the belief the war would be over within a few months.

At the front of the queue and arched over the table, signing a piece of paper was Mr Alderthay, the schoolmaster, or Hubert, as Drake insisted on calling him. Mr Alderthay was smiling when he rested the pen on the clipboard and straightened his back to shake the hand of the green clad officer beside him. Turning away from the table he saw Bertie and the gang and he waved, but within the moment and before they had time to wave back he had disappeared amongst bodies as those about him patted him on the back and cheered.

Newt innocently joined in with the clapping and praised Mr Alderthay for being so brave, but the girls worried for his safety and sympathised for his new wife, and her soon to be first child, however Drake sneered, and told them Hubert was not a fighting man and he was a fool for changing his chalk for a bayonet. Bertie, being quiet, did not join in the squabble.

Worryingly, he had seen James loitering amongst the men, reading pamphlets and staring at a poster with a drawing of a moustachioed man warning, *'Your country needs you!'* as he pointed out his stretched finger.

As the debate amongst the gang rumbled on and Millie and Lily voiced their worries about not being able to return to school, Bertie's eyes continued to stalk James and they followed him with apprehension as he talked, nodded and walked along the column until he eventually bored his way through the bodies to disappear within the smog of the Hound and Rabbit.

Chapter 4

As the autumns early darkness closed in to stop the playful merriment and adventures in the cove, Bertie, Finn, and the gang continued to gather every evening to sit, chatter and torment each in the disused Shepard's hut on the cliff top. Without the benefit of the long nights and warm weather, their activities mainly consisted of shooting stones over the cliff tops with their catapults, challenging each other with Yoyo tricks and huddling around a campfire to chatter. Scouring amongst the rocks and seaweed for treasure was now confined only to the daylight hours of the weekend.

Millie was disappointedly right about the school closing, and to make matters worse all the children had not been allowed to enjoy their idleness as a requisition officer had been in the area performing a survey of all things useful for the war effort and he had returned a week later with a small unit of soldiers to take away all the farmers horses. In the absence of the horses, the school children had been put to work in the local fields. Toiling in the soil and pulling rooted vegetables had replaced the mental activities of the classroom for the time being.

Their chatter was of all things meaningless unless you are 14 and under, began to mature into nervous anxiety as reports of adversities and catastrophes in France spread fast from the street corners to the kitchen tables. Suddenly, one night when hunkered around the campfire, everyone noticed Newt had developed a nervous stutter, which resulted in a self-imposed and uncharacteristic silence for a few days.

Eventually, after Millie's reassurances and sympathetic encouragement, it vanished just as quickly as it had started, albeit not before Drake had seen it as another opportunity to mock and ridicule him in front of the two girls. It wasn't until the following week that Lily found out and told the gang that Newt's father Billy, wanted to beat his older brother into enlisting, and so he fled the clutches of his wife's begging arms to become the first man in the village to volunteer for the chivalrous fight.

Drake didn't apologise for his cruelty, he had no need. Newt had taken to isolation for the winter and no one could persuade him to leave his room. In addition, Drake dismissed Billy Newton's courage by claiming that soon all their fathers would be taking up arms against the Germans. Both the girls gasped at the thought, and hoping he was wrong they looked at Bertie to correct him, but for once he ignored his friend's thoughtless jibe and kept his thoughts to himself as he poked the glowing ashes around with a long charred stick.

Within the Lanyon's small cottage and around the hue of the kitchen oil lamp, Bertie's Ma had continued to be her solemn self, enduring her grief whilst performing her duties in a morbid near silence. Every day she looked sadder and thinner and the dark skin under her eyes was a continual witness to the prevention of unaided sleep.

Every evening the ending of supper was marked by James reading out every line of the war reports in the grubby fingered newspaper. At first he enthused, along with everyone else, the British war heroes would push back the Germans by Christmas, and the war would be over by the end of the winter, however as the weeks sped by, his optimism began to wane.

Sitting rigid, both Bertie and his Ma would carefully listen to every word he lipped, and tonight with slow deliberation he spelt out a previously unheard word 'Zeppelin' and he told of German air bombings by these huge gas-filled balloons.

After a pause, James held up the page to show them a picture of the cigar shaped airship. They all contemplated the previously never considered damaged these weapons could inflict. Ma bit her fingernails, and sighing, she turned away. She'd been troubled enough for the night, and she needed solace, so reaching for the black bottle, she gave her boys a nod and headed for the stairwell.

Unperturbed, James watched her silently leave, and then spread the pages of the magazine out across the table to continue reading out the reports of huge losses of lives in France, and a statement from Lord Kitchener asking for another immediate 500,000 volunteers, which he repeated energetically.

Bertie's mind had also strayed. He was conjuring images of the Zeppelin high in the clouds with both wonderment and horror and so he didn't notice James tapping his chin with his index thinking as he considered the latest appeal.

By the following week James could no longer wait for the second hand newspaper to be passed over the backyard wall, and so he raided his savings tin to rush out and buy an old peddle bike so that on his journey home from work he could to ride into Trewin and buy the latest newspaper.

Over the following days both Bertie and his Ma noticed his eyes widen when the print repeatedly confirmed there had been a surge of volunteers up and down the country, and that newly formed units of fighting men had been proudly marching out of their hometowns to bands playing rallying pomp and Union Jack waving crowd cheers.

Ma had tried to quell his obvious enthusiasm by stating that amongst the splendour and the courageous there would be equally many wives, and children worrying, and wandering about the fate of their loved ones as they stared at the empty place at their tables and rolled over in bed to stretch out their palms on the now cold and empty side of the bed.

"All the gallantry and obligation, all the young men being driven along the same path with the same heroic end in sight. Not one of them caring or realising that the end may well be the forfeit of their life." She warned, rising from her chair to collect the cutlery and clear away the plates.

She was right, and they both knew it. She had, and still was experiencing the pain of loss, which would soon enact its evil toil upon millions more innocent souls. Unmoved by his Ma's obvious disdain, James continued every night to read out every column in full gruesome detail. A week later, he quoted that light restrictions were being imposed in all ports and government considered targets.

A few days further on, he announced that due to an air raid on London where innocent civilians had been killed, more drastic action was planned, and that street lighting in all areas was now banned with immediate effect.

26

"Won't bother us none." He muttered to himself, reflecting that their village had just one street light on the junction of what was once the main street. Then he smiled, recalling long gone were the days when the village folk would gather under it to gossip and pass on their good wishes before they quenched their thirst with a pint of the local brew in the now boarded up 'Ship Tavern'. These days, with no tavern and only a few South Cliff inhabitants still living in the village, there were no more gatherings and frolicking around the lamp post, only brief war chatter over the rear yard walls.

Bertie and the gangs routine stayed the almost same for the next few weeks. Bertie and Drake would rise early and go around the local farms to find work, but regularly now, with the field crops harvested, they would often end up joining the girls and help them to do chores at home.

Twice a week Bertie and Drake would saw up the wood they had amassed from the Cove and distribute it amongst the villagers to ensure their stoves were kept burning throughout the long miserable winter. Any leftover kindling would be bundled and barrowed for the girls to sell on their visits to Trewin, where they handed out scribbled notes stating they were competent sewers and available for undertaking garment alterations and repairs.

As usual, after supper and with just a hand full of coins for the wood, the girls would meet up on the cliff top to gather with the boys, however due to the national blackout and for fear of being seen by the Germans, they insisted the boys could not light their habitual fire.

To stop their bones from quivering Bertie suggested they should to make a base camp in Old Man Corney's derelict shepherd's hut.

27

Although two partially standing walls had survived the years of neglect and just four loose slats remained on the roof, the covering provided them with just enough shelter to keep the howling gusts from their backs and block out the light from the small campfires. After much debate with the girls and only after Bertie promised to seek out Old Man Corney's permission, the hideaway became the home for tales of dubious pirate exploits and ghost stories.

Later that cold month James purchased from Trewin's post office a pictorial magazine called 'The War Illustrated', and although berated by his mother for the outrageous cost of 2d, the magazine afforded him a greater knowledge and understanding of the complexities of the war. So enthralled was he by the new magazine with it's pictures, James was able to extend the supper time war briefings with more detail to include all the glory and the harrowing details of the soldier's woe in the face of the devilish enemy.

Chapter 5

As the winter waves swelled, and the tide hissed and thundered into the treacherous rocks dispersing it's cold and fearsome spray high, the gang's beach combing adventure had almost completely stalled. Ice glistened everywhere, and the air was so cold the small camp fire in their den no longer kept warm their hands and faces.

Bertie plucked up the courage to ask Old man Corney if he could strengthen the dilapidated hut and create a stronger shelter by using some of their surplus wood. After some chin scratching deliberations, and a grumble in which he advised the gang should find something more useful to do in their spare time, he agreed to the proposal under the condition that Bertie fixed up his chicken coop first. Bertie didn't mind, it gave him the chance to practice with his saw and chisel, and just one week later, under the dimness of the moon glow with frost numbed hands from the winter breeze's raw edge, he and his merry helpers had shored up the remaining walls from a pile of nearby rubble, added a wooden leant-to and laid a heavy planked floor. Completely covered the twenty foot extensive structure with a flat panelled roof consisting mainly of dismantled crates, once again the merry gang could chatter away the nights whilst being warmed and allow themselves to be temporary unburdened of war worries by the hypnotic dancing flames.

However, it wasn't too long before boredom began to set. They soon exhausted their knowledge of card games. Marbles no longer exited them, and playing with Newt's metal soldiers had lost its appeal long since.

Millie and Lily occupied themselves with knitting and made doilies from scraps of wool which they hoped to sell on their visits to Trewin. Drake still continued to irritate everyone this time by repeatedly slicing wood to create thin slivers which he would then hold for as long as he could above the flames, all the time looking at Millie, hoping she would take the bait and reprimanded him. Newt, remaining silent, sat between the girls, readily allowing them to use his hands as a wool spindle, but as a group they did little else.

Bertie resisted as long as he could sneaking out from the cottage 'The War Illustrated', but submitting to his urge to cut the boredom took the magazine from under James's bed, and began quietly to flick through the pages to digest the provoking reports from the radiance of the flickering firelight.

It wasn't too long before the rest of the gangs inquisitiveness became roused, and although fearful, and often dreading the reports, they also did not possess the will power to ignore any longer the importance of the war, and so like James did at supper time, Bertie also began the ritual reading out of the horrors from the weekly war report.

Soon enough, like the rest of the country the gang began to fear invasion, and their thoughts filled with dread, all assimilated from the lips of Bertie, and although they had little knowledge of Germany, they now hated the Boche and all things German.

Newt was the first to start it. He collected his entire, previously considered, fighting heroes, all poised ready for action in their grey uniforms and placed them one by one into the small furnace until the miniature soldiers had melted into small balls of lead.

Bertie followed by bringing an old metal racing car, and then Lily and Millie joined in the revenging sacrifices by bringing their porcelain faced Bavarian dolls. Of course, it was Drake's idea to burn them on a stake, Joan of Arc style. No longer, the gang declared, would they seek to find any pleasure from anything of German origin or made by the hand of the evil Germans. When the bittersweet patriotism ended, it was back to the pages of the 'The War Illustrated' to digest every enthralling yet gruesome and fearful detail.

"What's the VTC?" Lily asked.

"Voluntary Training Corps." Bertie replied. "Sort of a defence force made of retired soldiers and policemen whose duty it is to watch out for sneaky Germans."

"Sneaky Germans?" Newt looked up from the flames.

"Watch out?" Lily frowned.

"Sneaking on shore and spying for the Kaiser." Said Drake, jumping to his feet to peek out of the glassless window.

"Wonder if we'll get any?" Newt wondered out loud.

"Retired policemen?" Drake laughed.

"No." Newt shook his head. "Germen spies?"

"Not out here." Lily stretched to her feet and moved alongside Drake at the window. "There's nothing for them to report here." She asked him unconvincingly as she too frowned out into the darkness.

"Exactly! It's an ideal landing spot." Newt swerved the flames to pull back the tatty curtain they'd hung as a door. "Small empty harbour with no troops or navy boats for around miles." He pointed towards the old harbour. "They'd slip on shore and be away to the fields without anyone noticing."

"We could watch out for them." Millie suggested.

"Yes. We could be VTKs." Newt dropped the curtain and returned to the warmth of the fire to rub his hands together above the flames.

"VTCs." Bertie corrected. "Maybe not officially. We're too young, but we could do it."

"What?" Drake scowled. "Do what?"

"We could watch out for them." Bertie smiled at Newt.

"Yes. We'd notice them. Nobody knows these cliffs and coves like we do." Newt leaped beside Lily to join her scanning the black horizon.

"We'd have to have a name and make our own uniforms." Millie enthused.

"Oh, yes." Lily excitedly clapped her hands. "Maybe the ladies of the sewing club in Trewin will help us."

"We'll need a name and an insignia." Bertie urged.

"An insa?" Newt turned to ask. "What's an insssss...g...a

"Insignia's. It's a type of badge to show everyone who you are. The Voluntary Training Corps has a brown one with the letters GR." Bertie explained.

32

"Great Reservists?" Drake eagerly added with a huge grin..

"No. I think's its Latin for Georgius Rex." Bertie corrected.

"Oh, aren't you the clever one." Drake slammed, noticing Millie's eyes widen as she stared at Bertie.

"Not really. Our James told me." He grinned holding up the magazine to show a picture of a line of overweight, middle-aged men saluting.

"I don't want to be one of those if they are anything like that awful requisition officer who invited himself in for a cup of tea." Lily recalled the abhorrence which was similarly shared around the kitchen tables, street corners and ale houses throughout the country. "Pretending to be all friendly and turning out to be horridly mean and cruel."

Even though everyone knew the Germans needed to be stopped by all means necessary, there had been an overwhelming out pour of sympathy for the innocent four legged land workers who did not know how to duck from a bullet or take cover from a German shell. The remainder of the miserable month passed by with a mixture of good and bad news. Newt's Pa had sent a brief letter home to confirm he was in good health and stating the loved ones he left behind should not worry or distress too much.

However, the general reports in the press and in 'The War Illustrated' confirmed all the early optimism had now well and truly been banished, as now there were first-hand accounts which detailed vast numbers of casualties and reports that being outnumbered, a great many of the British soldiers in France were now retreating.

Bertie's Ma, often shaking, frowned as she sat and listened to James's nightly dictations. She's seen him bite his lip, hold his breath and flicker his eyelids as though he'd wanted to say something, but after a pause and consideration he had succumbed to second thoughts. Nevertheless, it had not gone unnoticed by the widow, and she displayed the signs of worry as night after night she notice in the fervency of his tone he had begun contemplating thoughts of valour and courage, albeit ignorant of any competence. She didn't say anything to her eldest boy, but she'd make sure she'd do her damned best to stop him from enlisting. After all, he was still only 16.

Bertie understood his brother's desire for excitement. James was too old to join in the playful activities with the gang, and he wanted something more challenging than just joining the newly formed South Cliff Voluntary Corps, named by Newt's with Millie's quickly stitching SCVC on some old brown socks to make the gangs arm bands.

To make matters worse, there was no worthwhile work in the area, there wasn't anybody left in South Cliff of his age nor a nearby alehouse where he could drink away his pent up boredom. Both Bertie and his Ma knew it wouldn't take much to prise him away from the tedious emptiness.

Chapter 6

Fittingly, an icy gale howled along the single street village. It rattled the gates in the back alley and it pelted heavy rain against the cold glass windows when deliberately, after supper Bertie's Ma delivered the solemn news.

As with most teenagers, Bertie and the gang hadn't really considered death, especially not to someone they knew yet whilst around Europe it deprived thousands of a peaceful night's rest.

The dreaded 'deeply regret to inform you' telegram had been delivered to Mrs Alderthay informing her that her husband, the father of her new-born baby, and the local schoolmaster, who was last seen displaying a huge patriotic grin outside the Hound and Rabbit, had been killed in action.

The unfortunate Hubert Alderthay was suddenly and briefly famous, only in the way no one wanted. He was the first man in the parish to be killed in the great conflict.With rumoured falsehood spreading like the plague and wanting to oust all thoughts of heroics from her boy's imaginations, their Ma did not delay or moderate the dreadful news.

"Apparently, never got the chance to fire his rifle. Poor fellow, shot by a cowardly sniper." She did not break her stare from James for one moment as she rasped heavily. However, she did still worry the news may only stiffen his resolve. "You boys will have to come with me to the church."

James, although listening, did not at any time raise his eyes from the print of the latest magazine. "What? I never go to church."

He grumbled, turning the page. He'd just rather stand outside and lower his head instead of listening to God's justification for taking another man's life.

"We must pay our respects. Mrs Alderthay was kind to me when ….."

"A funeral without a body?" said Bertie.

"A remembrance. Like, you know ………" She sighed. "I expect there'll be a huge turnout and I want you two boys by my side." It was the first time she had spoken with any kind of spirit for months. "You owe it to the poor fellow. He taught you both well and without him you wouldn't be able to read out all those ghastly reports you trouble us to every night."

"Duke of Cornwall's Light Infantry." James confused her.

"What?" she scowled.

"I'm trying to see if there are any reports of Mr Alderthay's regiment."

"Somewhere near a place called Doullens." She looked over his shoulder and down at the open pages. "Not far from Amiens."

"Poor bugger didn't get very far." James tapped his finger on a drawing of a map." Nowhere near the western front."

"Like thousands more." She pitied.

"He knew the risks, didn't he?" It was a statement confirming he was mindful of the dangerous reality, whilst still disregarding his Ma's concerns.

By the time Bertie and Finn made it to the shepherds hut, now known to the gang as the 'Command Centre' because it sounded worthier and more fitting to their newly adopted roles as lookouts, all his friends had been subjected to the same conversation by their parents. Both Lily and Millie were teary-eyed and not in the least bit playful. They both liked Mr Alderthay and were surprised when they saw the polite mannered man at the front of the volunteers queue.

"How could the dastardly Germans take away the life of such a pleasant man?" Millie cried.

"Bullets and cannon don't discriminate." Drake insensitively stated.

'And neither do the waves.' Bertie wrapped his arm around Finn and resting his head on his silky back, he hugged his comforting companion. "God no longer cares." He whispered into Finn's ear.

The remainder of that night passed with only the noise of flame crackle fracturing the unusual silence. The dancing flames and prodding of the charcoal seemed enough to occupy the thoughts of the youngsters as suddenly and unexpectedly they had found being playful and jolly unappealing. Thoughts of making regulation uniforms and burning more German toys could wait a few more days.

The following Sunday, Bertie and James were roused before dawn. James dressed in his father's old suit and Bertie wearing James's old Sunday best they were to join the village mourners and pray for the soul of Hubert Alderthay, and offer their support to his young widow. Knee to knee and shoulder to shoulder they crammed in the back of Old Man Corney's cart to take the 7 mile ponderous trek to the church in Trewin.

Wrapped in blankets and scarfs, and with their brollies raised to shelter them from the perpetual unfriendly gusts of sleet and snow, in the half-light, the cart began swaying and shaking as the wheels rolled forward under the control of Corney and his old nag, the only one left in the county.

The journey was vividly reminiscent of the one taken only a few years earlier and considerations were given to the widow and the two fatherless boys, themselves without a body to mourn or a funeral in which they could lay to rest in peace their deceased loved one. Other than a few morning greetings, everyone clamped tight their mouths to deliberately avoid any comments about the dead man whose body lay far away from the Godly churchyard.

In near silence, the village mourners slowly made their way towards Trewin. The gang huddled tight against each other, heads and shoulders wet, backs cold and shivering they too along with the solemn adults cared little for needless words.

Upon reaching the large congregation who had gathered at the church gates, all void of spirit and heavy with damp clothing, their ears were met with the thunder of a drummer beating forth the call to prayer. Stood at his side and standing perfectly erect, and splendidly dressed in green uniforms sprinkled with snow, five officers with their necks stretched tall, removed their hats and saluted with regal grace the young widow as she was led by the arm up the slushy stairs and into the church.

The tribute by the soldiers was maintained, as quickly and silently the orderly queue of worshipers and mourners followed on behind to take up their positions on each side of the isle.

Then, without delay the beating stopped, and the doors were closed. Breath misted the air, and all whispering hushed as a solemnity bestowed upon the congregation, the only sound being the wailing from the front row and the rustling of turning heads as the officers tough leather soles marched a beat on the stone slabs until they took up their assigned positions next to the vicar and at the side of the bereaved.

Not lost on Bertie's mother, as she stole curious glances at the gathering, was the large number of unaccompanied wives. She knew who their prayers were for, 'Not my Ernest, thank you God.' 'Lord please take care of my Frank.' 'Oh God keep safe my George.' 'Oh Lord please no telegram today.' Understanding their plea's she closed her eyes and made her own prayers, all the time hoping James would not notice the lack of males companions.

With the sermon and songs finished, the vicar made a special tribute for the unfortunate former headmaster, and he ended the service with a prayer for world peace. Then, after a peaceful moment of prayers the congregation slowly filtered out behind the new widow with the same graveness that marked their entrance.

Bertie saw his Ma raise her head and touch the shoulder of widow Alderthay.

In her eyes, dullness lamented testament, she knew the widow was wasting her time praying, as yet still her own heart was pained from demons knowing God had turned his back once more. Bertie squeezed her hand and teary-eyed, she once more lowered her head to follow the noise of footsteps out of the church.

Within a few moments, her condolences were forgotten as she angered at the green clad officer with perfectly coiffed hair who was casually chatting and shaking the hand of James.

"Have you no shame." She screamed as she tugged James's sodden arm away from the smiling burly officer. "He's only 16!"

A mixture of outrage and anger had overtaken her sorrow for the unfortunate Mrs Alderthay.

"He's a big strapping fellow Missis……" He paused, waiting for her to offer her name, but when she ignored his cue, he added. "Our country needs plenty of big young men to fight the Huns and keep our shores safe from invasion."

"Men not boys!" Heads turned in the direction of the clamour that spread far against the wintry quietness, and James's face reddened. He pulled back against his Ma's vice holding grip, but shaking her head in disgust at the officer, she used every fibre to haul her boy away.

"Oh my." Millie took Bertie's hand and squeezed. "They should know better."

"James is stubborn and in the end, he'll only do what he likes." He replied.

Embarrassed, James raged at his Ma and resisted her force so violently to stay on her feet on the slushy cobbles she had no option, but to relent and release him from her grip. Cussing loudly, James barged his way through the stationary and bemused onlookers to disappear amongst the black shawls and raised umbrellas.

"You should be ashamed of yourself!" Bertie's Ma lambasted the grinning officer again, then adjusting her clothing quickly and raising her brolly, she turned her back to him.

"The boy has a fight in him Missus, and you'll not be able to repress it." He shouted back.

"You mustn't let him go Bertie." Millie warned. "You need to keep your eye on him for your Ma's sake. She won't cope with the thought of losing another loved one."

Bertie dismally shook his head and sleet dripped from his hair. "I'm scared Millie." He wiped his face. "I'm scared James has an itch that won't go away with just scratching."

Chapter 7

The menacing winter storms manifested for another eight weeks. Refusing to ease, the low-hanging clouds swept across the entire county, releasing a barrage of heavy snow that blanketed the ground with a dazzling whiteness that cut off all travel, isolated and silenced South Cliff.

At first, playing in the snow was fun. Finn leaped and bounded through the crunch. Snowmen lined the empty streets and brick everywhere was dotted with splattered snow balls from miss aimed throws. However, boredom soon beset upon Bertie and the gang, and in the short days where the light barely penetrated the dense white clouds, continual face stinging gusts hindered them from taking the perilous path down into Horseshoe Cove, and prevented them from scourging for anything, but the essential wood.

Old Man Corney generosity ensured the families of South Cliff didn't starve. Often he'd create unnecessary work for the few men of the village. Tasking them with repair work and livestock duties, but food was in short supply, and it was not long before everyone's stomach ached with hunger.

Once a week James, Bertie, Drake and Newt endured the endless blizzards, and large snowflakes which had piled up against the buildings, to trudge knee deep beyond the cut off village and make their way to Trewin to try to sell firewood, run errands and buy supplies which included the now mandatory 'The War Illustrated'.

Hidden beneath a layer of tarp, Drake and Newt reined Corney's horse and cart, and guiding from the front James and Bertie would shovel clear the unpassable deep drifts.

Late March, James returned from Trewin with a leaflet detailing the ladies of the congregation had formed a War Aid Committee and they were imploring the locals to send food parcel and blankets to the heroes who were also suffering in the extreme conditions overseas.

The folk of South Cliff had nothing to give, but Bertie's neighbour's organised a sewing club, and so a couple nights a week the women and girls of South Cliff, would gather around the stove's in each other's cottages to strip down old blankets and ragged clothing to knit socks, gloves and scarfs. Amongst the small group of women it was noticeable to all how excitable Millie seemed with Bertie, and how little she could focus on her needlework because her eyes uncontrollably glared at him as he, ignorant of her yearnings busied himself stacking wood for the stove and carrying back and forth old blankets and scraps of wool.

The sewing club distracted the widow from her pained memories, and occasionally her mood would brighten up, but as regular as day and night when the needles were packed away for another night she allowed herself to sink back into her deep sadness and reach for the black bottle.

Try as they only knew how, by keeping all talk of war within the confines of their bedroom James and Bertie could do nothing to ease her worries and her melancholy as the news of the thousand suffering on the front lines could not be withheld by the chatter of the sewing group or the neighbourly pleasantries over the yard wall.

As the harsh winter dragged on cruelly, all reports confirmed the Germans had intensified their efforts to repel the British advance and all hopes of an early ceasefire had now been abandoned. The government's plan was failing, casualties were high, and now reports suggested a mass evacuation was to commence.

James shook his head in disbelief as his finger traced along the line of letters, which confirmed thousands of deaths at a place called Ypres.

"They're coming." Lying on the bare bedroom boards with the newspaper spread in front of him, he tilted his head towards his Bertie.

"You hear me."

"Eh?"

"They're coming."

"What……. Who's coming?"

For once, he'd not been listening. He'd been twirling Finn's fur, and embarrassingly recalling how Millie unexpectedly stretched up to kiss him on the cheek as she waved him goodbye to follow her Ma out through the door, and into the biting cold. She'd never done that before and, sceptically, he hoped no one had noticed.

"The bloody Germans, the Bosch, the Huns, the sauerkraut munching ….. bastards." He banged his balled hand against the newspaper. "It states it right here. They're calling it 'a race to the sea'. All our boys have been forced to give up the fight and they're running for their lives."

"Invasion?" Bertie slumped to his knees and peered over James's shoulder to gaze down at the report.

"Were on the run and the Germans are following us quickly behind."

"Oh bugger." Bertie dashed towards the door.

"Where are you going?" James shouted.

"Command Centre. We need to watch out for them coming."

"Don't be daft. It'll be too dark to see anything."

Ignoring his brother advice, Bertie swiftly, but silently, and avoiding the creakiest stair carefully tread to grab his coat, scarf and hat to tiptoe quietly passed his sleeping Ma and to turn the kitchen door handle.

"Wait for me!" Less cautious James shouted as he bounded across the bedroom floor and leaped down the stairs, his feet barely touching the steps. However, entering the kitchen and seeing his Ma sleeping in her chair by the fireside, he did restrain his excitement enough to sneak out behind his brother without awaking her from her slumber.

With a great excitable urgency which shielded them from the freezing wind, the brothers raced and slipped their way across the untouched white covered cliff tops until gasping out clouds of hot breath, they halted with unexpected disappointment.

Bertie's jaw dropped, and his misery prevented any utterance. Destroyed by the fierce gales, the Command Centre was just a pile of snow covered rubble and timber.

He dropped his head into his hands and blowing to warm his fingers, he cussed his lack of skill. James laughed and teased his brother for his incompetence, but noticing Bertie's lack of humour and despair he slapped him on the back, and told him as soon as the snow began to clear they would return, and together they would build a bigger and much stronger den which would be capable of surviving the meanest of gales.

With nothing to see except darkness, and without shelter, suddenly the cold hit them, and so after patting the sides of their bodies to warm themselves a little, they once again sped through the snow, this time in the direction of home.

The great thaw couldn't arrive quickly enough for Bertie and the gang. Dismal, and fearing invasion, their pent-up frustrations could only be eased by the distraction of James's promise to reconstruct a stronger Command Centre.

The washed up winter debris on that first Saturday in April thrilled the playmates, albeit for only a few minutes. Shock had briefly muted them as overlooking the Cove from the windy path, in awe, their gaping eyes feasted upon the storm blown bounty below.

Planks, crates, bottles, and undistinguishable treasures were strewn in huge quantities around the curve of the small beach and wedged between the mass of rocks which lay at the base of the steep white cliffs. Wasting no further time, they skipped and slid down the narrow path into Horseshoe Cove to make the most of the weekend's gloomy light.

James being determined to fulfil his promise and rebuild the den, took charge of the operation. No one dare object to his commands, and they all conducted their duties with military veracity. Although they all were glad of James's commitment, a little sadness tinged their joy. His mere presence ensured there could be little time for playfulness, no foolery, and to Newt's delight, no teasing about his stammer, which had worsened throughout the bleak hibernation. However, the gang spirits were cheerful, and they were relieved the winter's tedium had finally come to an end.

They filled their lungs to the full with the salty cold air, and sang as they worked, and without stopping for a rest they skipping up and down the path with their arms laden heavy with timber until the early sunset interrupted their long waited, yet welcomed toil.

All undamaged crates were neatly stored in the cave, only to be opened once the new build was complete, and all the timber was relayed to the cliff top. Day by day the boys repeatedly hauled, and dragged wood up from the cove, as Millie and Lily keeping out of their way, rummaged through washed up debris to salvage items such as candles, blocks of fat, paint, oil cans, bottles of beer and soap.

"We must help protect our country". James urged them on and repeated to Bertie, Drake and Newt as out of breath they lumped huge lengths of shattered timbers up the winding slippery path from the rocks, until finally at dusk and the shivering of their aching bones dictated it was time for a rest.

As the sunset to their right, they sat and chattered on the cliff top enjoying the rewards from their 'war efforts'.

The grinning boys, with fuzzy heads had clamped their blistered hands around beer bottles for the first time and swigged empty the flat strange tasting brew, whilst watching with interest, the girls laughed and joined in the tipsy joshing all the time doing their best not to get distracted as they sorted out their bounty into bundles for sharing out amongst the villagers.

Gradually, as each day lengthened, the piles of wood increased until finally James announced it was time to begin the real burdensome work of construction. In return of supplying Old Man Corney with several crates of beer, James arrived at the site of the ruin with permission for the rebuild and a barrow laden with carpentry tools.

Taking charge as expected, he gave orders for the girls, and Newt to dismantle the collapsed ruins whilst he and the older boys measured, sawed, chiselled and planed lengths of wood.

Newt, soon exhausted, was excused from his duties under the agreement he remained alert enough to watch out over the watery horizon for invading German ships. Occasionally the old man hobbled across the fields to visit his decrepit shepherds hut and check on the welfare of the gang, but James had anticipated his guise and artificial inquisitiveness, and knowing he was just snooping for more beer he wisely kept the washed up crates safely in Quintal's Cave along with the rest of the gangs considered valuables.

Soon the shoots of spring prettied the green baize of the cliff tops and the milder fragrant breeze increased James's fervour for completing the lookout post.

Solid pillars were deep-rooted to provide strength. Miter, mortice and tenon joints secured the corners and provided a sturdy frame for overlapping slats to be fixed along the extended perimeter walls. The original wall cobbles and other large pebbles were used to provide a solid floor, and the smaller oddments of broken and sawn crates were fixed to enable the fitting of a sloping shingle roof. Completing James's masterwork and the gang's hard graft, rolled tarp hung above the four window spaces and acted as a draft protector for the crude windows and doorway.

At first, the cliff top curiosity which stood out against the purple backdrop of the descending spring sun attracted the attention of the dozen or so village folk. Eager to see why night after night their children had returned home blistered and exhausted, they inspected the bare and unremarkable creation, and when satisfied there was nothing significant to see or concern them, they soon became bored and returned to the comforts of their fireside arm chairs.

Finally, when the prying eyes and inquisition had ceased, and veiled by the onset of the early evening dimness, the gang began to transfer some of their collection from Quintal's haunted cave to their new Command Centre. Empty crates provided the seating, treasures from the crates the entertainment, and sea battered candles and a makeshift brick stove the heating and lighting.

James found pleasure in simply lounging in front of the fire and gulping down the beer, but the rest of the boys were glad to forfeit their allocation, remembering clearly how they were plagued with a headache after following his lead on the last occasion.

Each, in turn, would take Finn with them for protection and watch out for German ships. Every half hour, they bravely walked along the cliff top to look down and inspect the abandoned harbour in the adjacent bay to Horseshoe Cove for suspicious activity. Millie volunteered to double her watch by accompanying Bertie when it was his turn, much to Drake's obvious irritation, and then to incense him further when her turn came around she refused his offer of companionship, and denied him the opportunity of being her chaperone by stating Finn was more than an adequate escort.

By the end of the first week, all the beer had disappeared and so had James. Without any beer to interest him, the gang's playful buffoonery soon bored him, and he once more consumed his time by scrutinizing the dailies and 'The War Illustrated' away from his Ma, and in the seclusion of his bedroom. But, undeterred by the departure of their fleeting leader the gang continued to meet in the Command Centre every night, perform their look out duties for the King, and they'd lose themselves in a world of bloodshed, and fearful invasion as Bertie read out the latest news from James's copy of the 'War Illustrated'.

Chapter 8

James smashed his clenched fist hard against the table top. The thud rattled the table cutlery and caused his Ma shudder. Upon seeing the headline in the newspaper, he forgot his rule of reading about the upset of the war in the presence of his Ma.

"Bloody Huns!" He lambasted.

"Language James." His Ma turned from the sink and steadying her grip on the pan of steaming broth which she nearly dropped as a result of James's unexpected outburst, she walked over to the table.

"Well, the buggers have only gone and sunk a liner." He cursed.

"Passenger ship?" She neared the table, rested the pan on a towel, and, after a short pause, muttered. "Why in God's name are they attacking passenger ships?"

"Cowards." James shouted, cutting off her mumbling.

"Where?" Bertie asked.

"Somewhere in the Irish sea. Friday 7th May." He continued, his voice drifting into a hush as his fingers traced the letters on the page. "L-U-S-I-T-A-N-I-A. Over 1000 dead in U boat attack."

"Christ!" Bertie's shock dictated his reactions.

"Language!" His Ma frowned, and with shaky hands she began to ladle the broth equally into the bowls.

"Bloody hell!"

"James! Language. I won't tell you again."

"But, Ma 300 of them were children."

"Oh, my ....no .... no. What has this war come to?" She dropped the ladle into the empty pan and slumped with a sudden onset grief into the chair. "Children." She sighed, raising her smock at the same time as lowering her face to shield her wet eyes in the material.

"We'll' not stand for it." He slid the paper across the table in Bertie's direction. "They'll not stand for it."

"We? They? What do you mean?" Bertie asked, opening his eyes wide at the artist's sketch of the sinking ship.

"They'll be a massive outrage. A resurgence of volunteers all willing and eager to get at the Hun." James slid back his chair. "And the Yanks."

"Yanks?" Bertie repeated.

"Yeah. There were some Americans on board." He looked out of the window towards the sea as if scanning for warships. "They'll want revenge. I'm sure of it."

"Oh, no." Their Ma sobbed into her clothing. "Too many have died already. Why can't they just make peace?"

"Too late now Ma. The Huns must pay." James sprang from his chair and pulled open the kitchen door. "And pay they must."

"And will." Bertie muttered.

"What about your food?" She shouted as the door slammed.

"Sorry Ma. I've lost my appetite." He shouted through the glass as he dashed by the kitchen window.

"If we didn't already hate them enough." Said Bertie watching his Ma's trembling hands grab the towel to wipe the spilled broth.

The remainder of that terrible weekend passed by with Bertie, and the gang on high alert for suspicious activity. With their resolution for watching out for dastardly and cowardly German warships strengthened, they stoically took up positions on the cliff tops overlooking the harbour and sea.

On the Sunday afternoon Newt arrived with a pair of binoculars, and stating he would be able to see U boat periscopes, he dared to climb the roof of the Command Centre to improve his view. However, the monotony of vigilance had exhausted the young guardians, and by late afternoon, their fervour and determination had waned. Enticed by the ebbing waves to wander down into the cove, they spent the remaining daylight hours searching amongst the rocks for crabs and debris.

Arms laden with fresh crabs for supper Bertie and Finn were the first to lead the way along the slope and return to the village, and nearing the rear yard Bertie heard his Ma talking to a man with deep toned voice.

He halted his stride, and grabbed Finn's collar to hold him back, then standing with his back pressed against the yard wall, he twisted his neck and angled his ear towards the voices. He did not recognise the tones of the stranger who was bidding his Ma goodbye, and his curiosity began to prevail over his wisdom.

Hoping to hear more than just a 'good bye', and find out why there was a stranger leaving by the rear yard gate, Bertie held his position, and ignored the increasing sound of leather soles crunching on gravel until the gate screeched open.

Acting unconcerned, but hiding the crabs behind his back, Bertie smiled at the olive clad soldier who arched low to reach out and pat Finn on the head.

"Nice dog you got there, boy."

Finn growled and shuffled backwards against Bertie' body.

"What's his name?" Asked the soldier, then he quickly retracted his hand and straightened his back.

"Finn." The soldier's face looked familiar.

The soldier scowled and seemed to hesitate. "Finn you say?"

"Yes, sir." Bertie replied in a wary whisper. Wondering why the soldier had come out of his home.

"Are you Irish?" The soldier tilted his head and stared at Bertie as though he was conducting an examination.

"No." Bertie frowned. He assuming and fearing the soldier was looking for James.

"Catholic?"

"No." Bertie was confused.

"Oh.....with a name like Finn, I thought your Pa might be a paddy." The soldier narrowed his eyes sceptically.

"No. It's Finn from the book Huckleberry Finn." Bertie exclaimed, wondering if or why the soldier was interested in his dog.

"Ahh, I see. That explains it then." The soldier ruffled Bertie's hair. "I don't care too much for the Paddy's."

"Paddy's?" Bertie shook his head.

The soldier lowered his head level to Bertie's ear and hissed. "The Irish, boy. There are all loudmouth anti-establishment troublemakers."

"There aren't any around here." Bertie nervously clarified.

"And long may it stay that way, boy. Now I haven't got time to chatter." He smiled. "Must be on my way. Plenty to do and little time to do it all in." He firmed his hat on his head. "Well boy, you take good care to look after... Finn, you say."

Bertie did not reply.

The soldier winked and turned to walk away. Bertie heard him repeat Finn's name, then whistling, he marched away at pace and turned the corner to disappear out of view.

"Ma! Ma! Where's James?" Bertie yelled as he burst through the door, throwing the crabs into the tin sink.

Shocked by the sudden intrusion Bertie's Ma gasped and dropped a leaflet she had been reading. "James?" She panted.

"Yes James. Has he…" Bertie did not finish his question because his attention was seized by the picture of a dog wearing a white vest with a Red Cross on the back. He picked up the leaflet and read the lettering 'Royal Artillery War Dog Training School'. His Ma turned away from him and looked out of the window over the fields towards the dark grey sea.

"You're sending Finn away!" He wasn't asking a question, he was angrily shouting. "To France! To die!"

"No, no." Turning to sit at the table still she avoided looking at Bertie. "The Lieutenant said the army uses dogs to carry first aid kits to injured men."

"I hate that man." Now he recalled seeing him. He was the soldier who visited the village a few months ago. Armed with a pen and clipboard, he inspected livestock, farming equipment and the barns. "First the horses, now the dogs." Bertie screwed up the leaflet and threw it into the fire.

"The Lieutenant told me the army is in desperate need of all the help they can get."

Her eyes fixed on the burning leaflet, she ignored her teary son.

"He has been particularly seeking out Retrievers. He said they are the most suitable breed for quick learning. Brave, adaptable and very clever……. And they take very well to the training."

Using her fingers as a comb, she feathered her ruffled hair back from her forehead. "And if he proves suitable."

Finally she raised her head, but not to look at Bertie. She reached out to stroke Finn's forehead, and he wagged his tail, opened his mouth and tilted his head, confirming he wanted more.

"Which I am sure he will be........ he may be trained to carry signals along the front line." She obliged him and rubbed a little harder. "Absolute vital work."

"You can't send him." Bertie pulled Finn away from her. "I'm not going to let you." He kneeled beside him and hugged him tight. Finn pressed his heavy head into Bertie's chested, and looked up, his eyes wide and sad, his rare caramel coloured nose puffing. He didn't know he was being sent away to danger. He just didn't like it when they shouted at each other.

"How can you even think of doing this?" He dropped his face into Finn's furry chest. "You love him.... Don't you?"

"We all must do our bit for the war effort."

"He's our pet." He hugged him. "He won't understand machine guns, shells or gas."

"The Lieutenant is an expert at training dogs. He said Finn would make a good messenger."

"He's not going. I'm not going to let them take him." Bertie stood and grabbed Finn's collar. "You mustn't let that soldier come near again." He led Finn to the hallway door. "How could you even think it?"

"The army needs him more than we do."

"No! No! No!" He ran along the passage and Finn, wagging his tail excitedly joined in the fun. "I'm not going to let him go."

Bertie ignored his Ma's calls forbidding him to take Finn upstairs, and he scooped up him up onto his bed. Squeezing his best friend tight and crying into his fur, he promised Finn that he was always going to look after him and never leave his side. No one was taking him away, he was not going to let them take him, and he'd go to jail if he had to.

Chapter 9

As expected, in Trewin fervour had gripped the hustling clamour of people who attended the first summer market day of the month. The war recruitment department had advertised their intention to take over the post office for the whole day over one week ago and since the advertisement had been posted, the talk amongst the gossipers had been about volunteering for the conflict and nothing else. 'Who was brave enough to go and fire a gun?' 'Who was bold enough to enlist?' 'Who was man enough and courageous enough to stand and fight in the face of death?'

Unlike the previous visit of 'the body snatchers' as Bertie's Ma called the officers when she overheard James and Bertie discussing the announcement, the spirit of the men in the long queue was not so jovial. Although they still bellowed out boasts bursting with patriotic optimism, their mood reflected one of grim sheer hate for the Hun, and a determination to put right their evil wrong doings.

Bertie's Ma was gladdened when she scanned the pallid faces in the line of volunteers. Not pleased that men were putting themselves in front of the devil, and sacrificing themselves so that others could live, but relived she had not seen James amongst the volunteers.

He'd risen before dawn and gone to work as usual that morning, but she's noticed in the passing month's an avoidance from him to discuss anything related to the war, and now within him an unusual sullenness had quieted his mood, burdening her with a fear that he was contemplating something she knew he would not deny and not discuss.

An unwelcome shuddered chilled her as she hesitated, turning her back on the naïve patriots. She turned her face in all directions, and squinted as she imagined James peering out at her from behind a market stall, or from the murk of a dark alley. However, all she could see was women and small children busying themselves their men folk lined to the front of her, yet again still she doubted her eyes and once more she delayed her exit to scrutinize the shadows, shop windows and doorways.

Bertie welcomed the warm sun and long nights with appealing enthusiasm. As arranged, exactly on time the gang met at the Command Centre to split into two groups and take up their new rota duties Split into groups, one would stay inside to watch out for suspicious activity on the seas whilst the other searched amongst the rocks of the cove for treasure.

In the bliss of the calm, and barmy evenings, they'd stay out as late as they dare collecting stockpiles of wood, glass, rope and occasionally unbroken crates which, in the secrecy of the Command Centre, they would open together.

The thrill and tingle of surprise never bated, and with fingers crossed, hoping for valuables, they'd crowbar open the bashed crate lids. In a short time, they'd accrued a pile of broken crockery, glass and unidentifiable parts of machinery.

However, occasionally they'd crack open a collection of various beers, tinned food and wines, and again, as before, they'd agree to share out their wealth amongst their parents and Old Man Corney. One treasure they found difficult to share out was a crate of damp chocolate bars.

Although wet and no longer shiny perfectly brown, the chocolate still tasted good, and it was only when their stomachs cramped and they felt sick from over indulgence did they take back to the village the crate to distribute the remaining damp bars.

Millie always seemed to be partnered with Bertie and Finn, and whilst taking a break from their obligations, together they enjoyed the passing hours chattering, swimming and tormenting Finn, all under the scrutiny of Drake who easily bored with his lookout duties, allowed his binoculars to angle down from the horizon into Horseshoe Cove and upon his friends. Here to his increasing angst, he'd ignore Newt and Lily's childish prattle, and gawk hour after hour at his desirous intended who was enjoying herself too much, and standing far too close to his best friend for his liking.

Although he dare not speak out about his jealousy, everyone felt his meanness. He'd ridicule Newt for his stutter, refuse to share the binoculars with Lily, and slacken from his duties, choosing to skim pebbles across the surface of the sea instead of searching the beach.

On other occasions, he occupied himself by lining up empty bottles and fire pebbles at them with his catapult. Later that summer, without inviting the others to join the fun, he attempted to brew a cask of scrumpy.

One evening Drake's petulance annoyed Bertie so much that after another bout of teasing Newt, he threatened to bloody his lip and, as usual, refusing to be humiliated in front of the girls, Drake reacted by releasing a tirade of insults upon them all.

Within an instant, the boys stood face to face with their fists clenched, and their chests expanded, exchanging threats and barging each until the girls forced their way in between them to halt the stupid bravado.

Fuming with rage born from embarrassment, Drake kicked over his barrel of apples, threw into the air 'The War Illustrated' and stormed out into the sereneness of the dusky late summer night to trudge miserably home. The confrontation upset the girls and Newt, but Bertie, as calm as ever, told them by the morning it will all be forgotten and the boys friendship would return, just as it always did when their stupid egos overruled their sensibility. However, still unnerved by the incident Newt said he wanted to go home, and hearing Newt's groan Lily immediately stopped calming Finn, and jumped to her feet volunteering to be her younger friends escort across the field, whilst Millie bearing a huge smile offered to stay behind, and help Bertie clean up Drake's mess.

An hour later, the couple creaked open the Command Centre door to step out into the near pitch of the late night when suddenly springing out from around the corner of the shack with a gruesome roar was a huge fluttering white manifestation.

Millie screamed "Ghost!" so loud that she alarmed frantic field birds to rise and flutter from their nests, and Finn growled so fervently that Bertie had to grab his mane to hold him back with all his might.

The moon glowing exposure groaned again and waved in front the static, loose jawed and shocked couple before disappearing back around the corner of the Command Centre just as quickly as it had appeared.

Millie spun and leaped to wrap her arms tight around Bertie's rigid body and, releasing his grip on the dog to hold her, Finn leaped forth into the darkness to chase the apparition.

Bertie could feel Millie's heart beating against his own pounding chest and, although he wanted to chase after the ghost, he knew he could not leave the distressed girl alone in the dark. For a brief moment, they both held the embrace, then realising their closeness and the tenderness of the hug Bertie, to hide his embarrassment, eased a gap between their bodies and began to laugh. Confused and displeased by his behaviour, Millie frowned and, folding her arm across her chest, she demanded to know why he found it so funny.

"Can't you see that was Drake?" He pointed out into the darkness.

"What?...... No.......It's the ghost of Quintal the pirate." She quivered.

"Quintal? No silly. It's just Drake being Drake." Reassuringly, he dropped both of his hands onto her shoulders. "He's just getting his own back by trying to scare us."

"Drake?" She trembled.

"Yes. It's his way of making us look foolish." He explained. "Come let's go and see."

"No." A flicker of moonlight revealed the terror on her face. "I'm scared."

"Don't be." Gently he squeezed on her shoulders. "Come on, it's going to be alright. Finn's probably got him pinned on the floor by now."

His smile began to ease her fear. "I promise you."

He lowered his hands and once again a crease appeared on her cheeks as she gripped tight his palm to walk by his side.

Bertie was still smiling about Drake's antics when he opened the door to enter the kitchen. He'd patted and rubbed Finn, who had quickly returned to Bertie with a mouthful of white fabric hanging from his teeth, and together they'd walked Millie home laughing hysterically as they walked across the cliff tops glancing in the darkness for Drake, or the discarded white sheet. However, even though they were sure he'd be watching and giggling somewhere not too far away, they found nothing and a small part of Millie still wondered if she'd seen Quintal's angered spirit.

Bertie enjoyed being Millie's saviour, and that night he sensed she wanted to kiss him as he wished her farewell that night, but fearing his own failure, he shied away from her pouting mouth, and pretended to be oblivious to her yearning. He'd never kissed anyone since he'd been a baby, only Finn and kissing Finn's mane and slabbering chops didn't give him the confidence he needed to lean forward and kiss Millie on her lips. He wanted to, he liked her and he cussed himself for not taking the opportunity whilst they were both lost in the moment of exhilaration, but he hadn't and he now regretted it.

Shaking his head as he opened the kitchen door he wondered if there would ever be a better time, and if there was, he vowed there would be no dumb excuses for flinching.

Closing the door behind him carefully so he didn't disturb his Ma, suddenly his alluring contemplation, and his matching smile banished as awake crying in her chair, his Ma bawled out.

"He's gone Bertie. He's gone."

She cast her reddened bleary eyes and paled face towards him.

"Gone?" Bertie scowled as he bolted the door behind him.

"He's gone and done it." She waved a crumpled piece of paper in her hand.

"What?" He stared at the crumpled note in her hand as he neared the table.

"Enlisted! He's only bloody gone and enlisted." Tears dripped from her face, splatting her already wet lap.

"James!" Bertie lifted the note from her hand and unfolding it he slumped into the chair opposite her.

Dear Ma & Bertie

I'm sorry to have to leave home this way, but I knew it would be the only way I would be allowed to serve my country. I think I can make a real difference and make you both real proud of me. Besides, the money will come in handy.

I'll take good care of myself, and I'll be sure to write often.

All my love James.

"How could he do this? How could he be so bloody stupid?" She dropped her head into her hands and sobbed uncontrollably, knowing his age and innocence had denied her the tender farewell she needed.

"Well, I guess the army needs all the help it can get." He repeated her words from earlier. There was no malice intended. He wasn't thinking clearly.

"Oh, please God, help us." She cried with little faith.

Chapter 10

Although the girls had decorated the Command Centre with pressed dandelions, daises and forget-me-nots, and hung a picture of the king above the door, the merriment within the group just wasn't the same anymore.

Bertie was slowly becoming void of all humour. Alongside his concerns for James, his Ma's melancholy had worsened. Sleepless nights and constant distress aged her, and day by day the circles under her eyes darkened and the worry lines on her forehead deepened. All conversations between them were almost none existent, and she went about her business of cleaning the house and cooking in a trancelike malaise all the time drinking bottle after bottle of her neighbour's homemade anguish remedy.

Bertie did not mention the war, nor dare he tell her about the names on the lengthening list of casualties which were now on display in Trewin's post office window.

Lengthy periods of silence now frequented the small cottage in South Cliff all too often, and on many occasions it was left to the all sensing tail-wagger to interrupt the awkwardness with his deliberate barks and attention seeking groans. Rubbing his face and snout on Bertie's leg, he knew full well the prompter for a good rubdown, and back scratch was the therapy for alleviating his master's heartache.

Drake had relented from his continual teasing of Newt, and to the annoyance of the girls who were desperately trying to concentrate on their sewing, he spent most of his time kicking a football against the wall of the Command Centre.

Subconsciously, his self-solitude and avoidance of all group activities was another tactic for gaining Millie's attention, one to which she was oblivious to.

The ghostly apparition was never mentioned again, mainly because the incident was darkened by the news of James's departure on the same evening, and so now the shrieking and screaming had lost its comical appeal.

Newt had not only matured throughout the now forgotten winter months, he had grown in height and was now almost at eye level with Lily. Playing with toys, and the girls no longer interested him either, and his sole focus became watching out for the dastardly German invasion force. Using the mainly discarded binoculars, he quietly, but devotedly scanned not only the choppy waters, but also he scrutinized the clear blue skies after learning earlier from one of Bertie's reading sessions that the Hun had now developed planes which were capable of carrying bombs.

Since the increase of U-Boat attacks on British merchant ship the government had begun to encourage everyone to start and grow vegetables, and so Millie and Lily, being determined to rouse the boys interest sought permission from Old Man Corney to use a small area of the land next to the Command Centre as a vegetable patch.

After a few moments of head scratching, chin rubbing, and grumbling. "The air's too salty. Nothing will root. Soils not suitable to grow veg." He eventually consented, but insisted. "I want 50% of everything grown."

For the best part of two weeks Bertie and Newt dug over the soil, weeded and sieved, and helped the girls plant seeds. Even beach combing had now lost it's appeal, and although they occasionally ventured down into Horseshoe Cove, after a little toe tapping against the side of the crates they soon found themselves distracted and looked for star fish, prodded jelly fish, dug trenches and recreated battles to pass time, their favourite being the capture of hill 60 in Ypres, where they would throw pebbles at imaginary German sharpshooters.

When the sun descended, and it was too dark to kick the football or scan the horizon, in the hue of candles Bertie continued reading the latest copy of the 'The War Illustrated' to absorbing ears, however his thoughts often drifted far away, wondering where James was and why he hadn't written home.

"It's very strange." Millie rested her hand on top of Bertie's. "You must be awfully worried."

"Is not like him." Bertie shook his head. "He said he would write." His eyes seemed to enlarge. "And I really thought he would."

"I'm sure he is safe." She squeezed his knuckles. "The authorities would have contacted by now if …" Imagining the worst, she deliberately looked away to prevent Bertie seeing the damp appear on her eyelids.

"Ma doesn't say anything. She won't even talk about it." There was a noticeable flutter in his tone, and to hide his own embarrassment, he arched to rub the back of Finn's ears. Finn's mouth opened, and his tongue dropped down by the side of his mouth. He groaned and wagging his tail he pressed his head against Bertie's hand, demanding more as he shuffled up tight against his legs.

Listening carefully, Drake suspected Bertie was exaggerating his woes just to gain Millie's sympathy. "Well, who are all the letters from then?" He couldn't resist.

"What?" Bertie frowned. He didn't understand.

"You know." Drake said nonchalantly. "No one in the village has been getting as many letters as your Ma." He clamped his hand over Newt's shoulder, and then patted him hard. "Not even poor Newt's Ma gets as many from the post boy."

"Letters?"

"You heard." Drake slighted his head back and grinned. "Either someone is writing to your Ma or the post boy has gotten all sweet on her."

"What?" Bertie threw down the magazine, leaped to his feet and balled his fist ready to strike out and bloody Drake's agonistic mouth.

"Yes." Lily said innocently, without looking up from her embroidery. "My old Nan." Suddenly noticing all eyes staring in her direction, she hesitated and spoke quietly. "Saw the postie delivering to your house last Tuesday ………. and again this afternoon."

Bertie eased back on the bench. His anger now distracted by Lily's innocent after thought.

"She worried it might have been ………. well, you know." She began to fidget with the cotton and needle. "The telegram."

"I'm sure they must not have been important." Millie cut in, also nervously turning buttons on her blouse. "Or she would have said something."

That night Bertie did not link arms with Millie and amble jovially home with the gang. For the first time he led the way out of the Command Centre, and sped home without caution, running into the darkness, and through the long spongy grass of the cliff top.

She was staring into the dying charcoals of the fire as usual. Her mind was far away from South Cliff, and yet again her fingers were wrapped around the half empty back bottle. Bertie asked her if she was ok, but as usual there was neither a reply nor any flicker of acknowledgment from her blank glare.

"Any news from our James?"

The mention of her eldest son's name resulted in the quiver of her eyelids and faintest shake of her head that no one else except Bertie would have noticed

"Lily mentioned the post boy dropped by," He urged a response.

"No." She murmured without breaking her glazed eyes from the simmering grey ash in the stove.

"Strange." Bertie inhaled, his right hand tensed and resting on his hip, his left rubbing his chin.

"Nothings getting through." She muttered, raising the bottle to her lips. "So I'm told."

"So he hasn't been?" His eyes narrowed as he studied his Ma's face.

"Not whilst I've been in." Tiredness weighed heavily on her eyelids and her head began to tilt against the padding of the high-backed armchair.

"You been out?" He knew she hadn't. She had rarely left the kitchen since James's departure.

She didn't reply and her eyes closed. The effort of speaking had exhausted her. He folded his arms under his chest and shook his head.

"Lily must have made a mistake, then?" He lowered his face to her ear and shouted. "I said Lily must have made a mistake."

"Mistake?" She muttered as Bertie's loudness temporarily jolted her. "I guess so. After all." Her eyes partially cracked open. "A bit dizzy." And her eye balls rolled white. "That girl." Her head slumped, and she exhaled a long, restful breath.

Bertie shook his head once more, wondering what she was hiding. "Good night Ma." He took the bottle out of her hand and placing it on the table, he lit a candle which he held at arm's length towards the hallway. "Don't be late to bed."

Flicking off his boots as quietly as possible, he trod the creaking stairs, and then pausing and staring at his Ma's bedroom door, he listened for noise from downstairs. Drawing a long breath, he pulled back the creaking door just enough to allow him to angle himself through the narrow gap and into the darkness.

Again, he stopped and listened, but all he could hear was his heart pounding within his chest and the boards squeaking beneath his feet.

72

Carefully he rested the candle on the nearest chest, then nervously he bent to reach out, and slide open slowly one by one, the chest draws until finally in the bottom draw he gaped disbelievingly at a neatly piled set of envelopes. His fingers feathered across the top envelope, and he lowered his face to try to read the writing without disturbing the neatly stacked pile. A quiver ran down his spine, and his hands and legs began to tremble uncontrollably as he wondered what his mother was hiding from him. Dread almost overwhelmed him, but he could not prevent himself from knowing the truth.

He locked his shaking fingers on the edge of the top envelope and lifted it out from the draw into the yellowish spray of the candle. He clamped his teeth, wondering if it was the appalling telegram everyone feared and he angled the face of the letter toward the hue of the candle to squint at the lettering of his home address.

'James.' He mouthed as the letters gradually revealed themselves in the flickering light. 'James's writing.' He gasped with relief, and dropped to his knees, then clenching his hands tight, he closed his eyes and raised his face towards heaven. "Oh … thank you….. Thank you God." A tear ran down his cheek, falling onto the dry ink.

Chapter 11

The carefree and idyllic benignity of the previous summers had long since been banished. The fear of invasion worried the gang, and the gruesome reports of the war had ensured they no longer played cheerful games on the cliff tops or fabricated pirate stories in Quintal's Cave.

Every evening they still gathered in the Command Centre, assigned look out duties, and scourged the cove for sea debris. But for Bertie, nothing seemed as perfect as before. His Ma's deteriorating health troubled him, and every day he prayed that God would protect James from Hun devils.

In the two weeks which had dragged agonising by since he had discovered the bundle of conceal letters, he had not been able to return to the bedroom draw. His Ma's latest rupture of despondency had prevented her from leaving her bed and not once had she stepped beyond the kitchen door to invigorate her skin in the fresh breeze. Besides caring for his Ma, completing the additional household chores, and being thoroughly occupied with his work at the farm, Bertie's mind had been burdened with increasing worry.

Repeatedly he questioned why she was hiding the letters from him, and he wondered to what they contained. Every day when he returned home from work, he asked her if she had any news about James, and then when the same replies were muttered. "It must be the censures........No letters are getting through........ No news is good news."

He wondered what secrets she was hiding, and building the courage to confront her tormented him. He had several times decided to brazenly opening the draw, but then after seeing her pitiful face he had become overwhelmed with sympathy and repentance, and he cowered away from treading into her bedroom. Every passing minute, his knowledge of the concealed letters pained him to act oblivious. He did not know how much longer he could continue the deception.

Finally, when it was his and Millie's turn to keep lookout, and the others were scavenging amongst the rocks in the cove, he decided to reveal his secret.

"Why would she do that?" Millie lowered the binoculars and turned away from the sea to look at Bertie. All thoughts of the Germans vanished, and her eyes widened with compassion. "She knows you're desperate for news."

Bertie's throat tightened, and his mouth became dry. He did not like talking about his Ma's complications. Without answering, he lowered his face to the floor and shook his head.

"I don't understand." She pressed her hand on his back and rubbed in a circular motion between his shoulder blades.

"Me neither." He muttered.

"You don't think?"

Bertie raised his face, his worried eyes were glazed, and Millie quickly changed the dreaded connotation.

"Maybe he's hurt? Or possibly been captured?"

"I don't know." He drew a breath to compose himself. It had been a relief to share the burden of his knowledge with Millie, but talking about James's demise had unexpectedly overwhelmed him. He turned away from her and angled his face to the window to gaze out into the perfectly serene dark blue where the sky merged with the water. "It's as though she's hiding everything away. Almost as if the war doesn't exist." He leaned on the wall, opening a gap between their bodies. "What do you think I should do?"

"Can't blame her. I think there are plenty of worried mothers doing the same." Concentrating, she twiddled her thumbs. "We'll all be glad when this is over." She desperately wanted to help, and her mind flooded with insane ideas until finally she blurted out. "I'll talk to my Ma."

"No. You can't." Bertie immediately objected.

She moved to stand beside him. "Don't worry. I'll just tell her that your Ma's has worsened and,"

"You mustn't." He cut in, worried and embarrassed that their neighbour's would be thinking she could not cope with her chores.

"Bertie. She is lonely, and she needs help."

"No. I'm not going behind her back like that." He turned away from the window and walked towards the door.

"My Ma can help her."

"No. I'm not betraying her."

"Help get her back into the Sunday routine. Get her back into the habit of going to church again." Millie rushed.

"I don't know ….. Everyone is already gossiping about her." He paused in the doorway and looked across the fields in the direction of the village. "And besides, I think she has lost her faith in God."

"This isn't a betrayal, Bertie." Millie followed him. "It's helping her. Get her out of the house and meet with people who are suffering the same agonies." She raised her eyebrows. "It may help you both."

Then she paused to listen to Lily's and Newt's childish prattle. Any moment she expected to see their heads and shoulders rise from the cliff top. Drake grumbling, no doubt not too far behind.

"Nothing more than that." She added, noting the contemplation in his stare as she glanced in the direction of the chatter, and then back across the grasslands towards the village.

"Whist she's out, I could read the letters." He faintly mumbled after figuring out with the travel and prayers he would have plenty of time to read and then safely put back the letters without his Ma's knowledge.

"Exactly."

Her plan had finally dawned on him, and she smiled just as Newt saw them and waved excitedly. He shouted and launched into a sprint, and then Lily instinctively began running with him towards the Command Centre. Racing each other, they hoped that Bertie and Millie were waiting at the door to welcome them back from their exploration to eagerly study their new findings.

That Sunday's morning bright rays shone through the window and illuminated the bedroom with a warm orange glow which falsely radiated Bertie's pallid face.

Although he wasn't neither hot nor cold, he shuddered, and sweat beaded on his forehead as he looked down on the weather soiled envelopes he had carefully laid out in date order on the bed before him.

He sighed, thanking Millie's thoughtfulness. Her delicately organised plan had so far fulfilled its objective. A few days earlier Millie's Ma had knocked on Bertie's door to inform them of a special tribute and fund raiser which had been organised by the ladies of the War Aid Committee. The event was to be held immediately after the Sunday worship.

Although Bertie's Ma seemed unresponsive to the idea of attending, and she gave no indication whether should would attend or not, Millie's Ma had gone ahead with her daughters request and stubbornly knocked on the door once again earlier that morning to usher her into Old Man Corney cart to sit alongside the other ladies from the village to take the journey in to Trewin.

Bertie knew he had until mid-afternoon to scrutinise James's letters, and hopefully find out why they had been kept a secret. His fingers trembled as he guided towards the first envelope.

18ᵗʰ July

The paper shook in his fingers, his legs weakened, he felt sick and he need to sit on the edge of the bed to open the envelope and slide out the first letter with his shaking fingers.

Dear Ma & Bertie,

Nothing much to write home about, I'm afraid. The food is good, and the bed is comfortable, but mainly we've been occupied with mundane training drills. In the mornings we march and dig trenches and in the afternoons in the periods of extreme heat we are subjected to tactical instructions under the cool shelter of a huge tent.

Many of them here are young and uneducated, and have simply sold their soul for a few pounds. They care little for the training and are only interested in getting overseas to fight the evil Bosch, but I am, I assure you, absorbing every detail of the training knowing that one day my life might depend upon it.

Today ammunition supplies arrived, and are now brimming with enthusiasm for tomorrow we are to be given our first bayonet, and rifle practice.

Hope you and Bertie are well. Write soon.

Love James

Noting Tavistock as the dispatch address, Bertie carefully refolded the letter in its original creases and replaced it in the envelope, then after a moment's hesitation he lifted from the bed the next envelope.

21st August

Dear Ma & Bertie

I hope you received my last letter dated 18th June, for I have strangely had nothing in return whilst my comrades around me have all received correspondence from home.

I find this rather odd and hope that it is some sort of failure from the army postal service.

I am pleased to tell you I have now arrived in Boulogne, France, and I am lucky enough to be billeted in an old and unoccupied lodging house with a terrific sea view, just like home!!

Our journey thus far has been rather an exhausting and bilious one. We shouldered arms at 12 noon and marched to Exeter railway station, then three cattle carts and six hours later we arrived in Folkstone where we slept out under the moon until at 7am promptly we were mustered for dispatch overseas.We marched off without a wash or a decent breakfast, only progressing 800 yards when a whistle signalled our recall. How flat we all were, everyone swore. I later found out failed departure was due to the high wind and concern that the rough sea could break loose the mines and we might get blown to blazes before we even properly set to sail.

However the swell soon eased and the following day we were dispatched without further incident, the only harm being that I am now suffering awfully with queasiness to which the Captain has assured me it's only as a result of all the travelling and it will soon be forgotten once we are on the march on solid ground.

Please write soon.

Love James

The final letter was dated 10th September. Bertie's eyes skipped across the opening paragraph where once again James bemoaned he had not received any news from home, and again he questioned the efficiency of the army's postal service.

We are here now, getting very close to our destination. We were first told that we were heading to the Argonne, but after a rest for a few days at St Omer, we moved off the main route and onto a beaten track which has led us close to a place called Beauval, some 30 miles from the Arras front. We have been told that here we will get our first sighting of the Hun…. Hurrah!

We had a truly awful trip down. The wagons were slow and uncomfortable, and then we had to march in constant rain. We were all beat, with no sleep, and soaked to the skin. None of us had the heart for a 12 mile slog in the mud whilst being overloaded with bags.

A creaking floorboard in the hallway caused Bertie to stop reading and slant his head towards the doorway. He held his breath to aid his listening, but relieved there were no further sounds, he once more lowered his eyes to James's letter.

Please write as soon as possible and if you can send socks, cigs and chocolate. All the soldiers here are receiving parcels from home and they use the cigs and chocolate to trade for eggs and milk from the locals.

Love James

The remainder of the letters simply detailed the weather and his approximate location. He stated there was now a lack of any basic comforts. He moaned at his blistered feet and he wrote he was frustrated because as yet he had not seen nor been introduced the Huns.

Suddenly, the hinges on the door squeaked. James dropped the letter and jumped to his feet, and with his jaw agape, and his heart pounding, he watched the door inch slowly inwards. Every muscle clamped within his body and he could not breathe as he watched the door move slowly again.

"Finn!" He gasped, seeing the gradual emergence of the familiar caramel nose and furry snout.

"What are you doing up here, boy?"

The inquisitive Finn, pleased he had found his friend, nudged the door fully open and waggled to Bertie's side, his swinging tail wafting the letters into the air.

Momentarily unconcerned about the letters due to relief, Bertie wrapped his arm around Finn's mane and rested his chest against his back. Then he rubbed both his hands vigorously in all directions over Finn's fur, causing him to grunt and blissfully whine for more.

Kissing Finn over and over on the snout and forehead, finally Bertie ushered the dog out of the room and back down the stairs. Then leaving with stern orders for Finn to stay put Bertie returned to the bedroom to pick up from the floor, and neatly fold back into the envelopes James's letters.

Still wondering why his Ma had not told him about James's brief communications as he reached down to grab the last of the fallen letters, his attention was seized by another piece of paper and an envelope which had been placed under the bed. Unable to control his curiosity, he slid his hand along the floorboards and dragged the papers out from the darkness.

At first, he thought the papers might be a reply to James, but as he scanned the first line, his eyes gaped wide and he frowned.

20th September

Dear Sir/ To Whom It May Concern.

I wish to inform you, my son James Lanyon, who is currently serving as part of the 4th battalion, Duke of Cornwall's Light Infantry, enlisted under false pretences at Trewin on the 4th June. He gave his date of birth as 7th August 1894, stating at the time of his enlistment, he was 21 years old and would soon be 22.

When my son enlisted, he was in fact only 16 years old. His true year of birth was 1899, and at this time, he is still only 17. I enclose his birth certificate.

I would like to request that my son be returned home to England as soon as possible. He should not be in the army serving abroad because, as you are aware, the required age to join the forces is 21.

Yours faithfully.

Alice Lanyon (mother & widow)

Chapter 12

What reasons did his Ma have for hiding the letters? Bertie repeated the question for hours as he sat on the cliff top with his arm around Finn staring out across the calm wave-less blue. He could not understand. He did not understand and he could not figure out why his Ma had withheld James's news. The news that confirmed he was safe and in good health.

He'd asked her again, when she returned from church, but her reply was just the usual blunt and cold 'no news'. Confused and disappointed by her deceit, and to avoid blurting out what he had discovered, he'd left her alone in the house almost as soon as she had returned from Trewin. Slamming the door behind him he'd angrily raced Finn across the cliff tops to await the arrival of the others.

He'd been there, sat in the grass hours too early for the rendezvous, and now shivering from the autumn chill and bored with staring out to sea with nothing to think about except the letters, he'd wandered down into Horseshoe Cove to pass away the afternoon snooping amongst the rocks and throwing pebbles into the sea for Finn to retrieve.

Gratefully his efforts had been productive as one sealed crate amongst the many of battered and broken contained glass jars of peppermints and humbugs. He'd hauled the two jars to base camp, and satisfied himself by eating a handful of each, then with his mouth tingling from the mild burn, he once again made himself comfortable in the long grass at the edge of the cliff.

"Penny for them?" Mille eased herself down to the grass and snuggled beside him. So lost in his thoughts he hadn't heard her skipping through the grass.

"What?" She startled him.

"A penny for your thoughts?" She smiled.

"I think you'll be able to guess." He raised his eyebrows.

"Were they from James?"

He nodded.

"Is he …………?"

"Oh, he's doing fine."

She gasped relief.

"It almost seems as though he's looking forward to the darn wrangle."

"Have you said anything? Did you ask her why?"

"No." He shrugged. "Not really. I did ask her and she just shook her head as she did before."

"What you going to do?"

"Not sure. What can I do? I mean without her knowing I've been snooping in her room." He shook his head. "I don't want to make her any worse than she is. She's already drinking bottle after bottle of that bloody poison as it is."

"I don't know….. Maybe when the post boy arrives." She doubtfully suggested.

For a long moment there was a pause as together, but silently they pondered idea's. Finally Bertie turned his face away from the chilling sea breeze and looked down at Finn.

"I've got it." He said. "I've got an idea."

Millie nodded and raised her eyebrows urging him to tell.

"What you two whispering about?"

From his bedroom window Drake had watched Millie skip and dance across fields, twirling her dress as her hair blew around her shoulders, and he cursed Bertie when he saw her snuggle beside him in the long swaying grass.

"Nothing." Although startled Bertie quickly and calmly responded. "You want some Humbugs?"

Sneaking into the house, and as customary sliding from her loosening grip the black bottle, Bertie did not wake his Ma. Silently he placed the bottle on the table, and then he went into the pantry to cut off several small chunks of cheese. Pulling off his boots, he then pulled the stairwell door behind him, and tiptoed up the stairs with the cheese cubes in his palm. He paused at the bedroom door, and angled his ear down the stairs, then after hearing nothing, but silence he entered his Ma's darkened bedroom and kneeled at the side of her bed. After, another brief pause he slid his hand under her bed and pulled out the letter addressed to the army.

He rubbed the letter with the cheese and slid it back under the bed before silently walking backwards out of the room leaving a trail of cheese from the bedside to the door. Once out into the hallway he continued down the stairs again leaving a small portion of cheese on every 4th step. Suspecting he was up to something Finn was giddily waiting for him at the hallway door and sniffing the air he jumped up to greet Bertie slamming both his front paws onto his chest.

"Shush boy." Bertie whispered trying to calm Finn with a two armed hug, but with his nostrils expanding wide and sucking in the aroma of the tormenting cheese he wriggled and tried to nudge passed Bertie.

Shushing him again in his ear, and pressing gently his hands on Finn's back he urged the dog to sit, and complying to the demand with drool hanging from his mouth, Finn sat, wagged his tail and waited for his master's blessing for the game to begin.

"Ma." Bertie reached out to tap his palm gently his Ma's shoulder.

"Ma." He whispered. "Ma." He repeated with a louder call until she lifted her head and grumbled.

"Ma. It's time to go to bed."

Whilst Bertie was distracted awaking his drowsy mother Finn saw the opportunity to investigate the alluring smell, and he pulled open the door a few inches with his paw, and then seizing the moment he spun and wiggled through the small gap to hunt the cheese.

Yawning and stretching tall her back and her arms in the air, she finally muttered. "Oh dear I must have dozed off."

"Yes, Ma you have." Bertie heard Finn's paws scurrying along the bare floorboards, and he saw the gap in the doorway. "I'm going up. Are you coming?"

He then paused and imagined Finn sniffing his way to the letter on the floor, and he crossed his fingers hoping his plan would work and that Finn instead of just frantically hunting around the room for more cheese would pick up the letter.

"Guess I should. Just can't seem to shake away the tiredness." Rising from the chair she paused in mid-motion, her hands still gripped to the arm supports. "What in the blazes is that noise?" She looked at the ceiling. "Have let that darn dog upstairs again."

"Sorry Ma." Together they heard Finn scurry along the hall. "But it must have been you who left the door open."

Simultaneously, their heads swivelled to the open door.

"Finn! What are you doing up there. Come down here at once you bad dog." Bertie shouted through the small gap all the time looking at his Ma's doubting scowl.

"I was sure I'd closed it." She rubbed her eyes and shook her head. The clatter and rumble of pacing paws galloping down the stairs added to her confusion and trying to recall if she had closed the door or not, she dropped back into the chair.

"What the ... "Bertie feigned his surprise as Finn bounded into the door with excited force and ran into the kitchen with his tail wagging, and the letter hanging from his drooling mouth.

"Finn! Come here." He patted his thigh to reinforce the command. "Come here now." He shouted sternly as Finn's tail swing increased.

"Finn here now." He repeated several times whilst pointing a straightened finger down to his feet until finally Finn stopped his wild spins, and with bulging brown eyes upon Bertie he cowered across the kitchen floor to drop the paper at his feet.

Reaching down, but making sure his Ma was not alert enough to see him, Bertie rubbed Finn's forehead with several rapid circle movements, and then he scratched the back of his ears and whispered.

"Sorry boy."

"What's this?" Bertie wiped away the slobber with his sleeve and reached to take the crumpled letter from Finn's mouth.

"Give it here." Finally roused her eyes gaped wide as she saw Bertie open the letter and angle the paper towards the lantern.

"Ma?" He frowned lifting his eyes above the top of the sheet to view his Ma's anger whiten her already stern face.

"It's mine." Trying once more to rise from the chair she was now alert enough to understand what Finn had retrieved. "Give it here. It's private." She flicked out her hand to lash out and grab the paper, but anticipating her reaction by slanting his back just a few inches he quickly and easily avoided her attempt to snatch the letter from out of his grasp.

"Don't read it!" She shouted, knowing it was too late.

"Ma?" He lowered the letter. "You know where James is?" He glared into her eyes, not asking a question, but demanding an explanation.

"I said don't read it." She flustered.

"And I asked you a question." He slammed the letter hard onto the table. "You know where he is. Don't you?"

She sighed and slumped back into the chair to fold her arms across her chest. Then clamping her eyes tight, she held back the emerging tears.

"Ma!...... well ...... do you?"

She shook her head and lowered her face towards her lap.

"Has James written to us?" Ignoring her pain for once, Bertie persisted.

Shadows hid the tears, which began to roll down her cheeks and drip onto her apron.

"Ma?" Bertie lowered his tone and knelt beside her chair. "James has written home? .... Hasn't he? ......You know where he is, don't you?"

She didn't answer, instead she sighed and drew in a large miserable breath, then shaking her head, she took a hold of the lantern in her shaky grip and walked out of the room and into the hallway.

Bertie didn't try to prevent her from leaving, instead he followed her to the door and shouted into the dark. "He has, hasn't he? Is he safe?" His words echoing around the empty stairwell. "Ma what's going on? Answer me."

He patted the confused dog that had followed him into the darkness.

"Good boy Finn. Good boy."

Eventually, she reluctantly answer. She returned to the kitchen, clutching the letters from her bedside chest in one hand and the lantern in the other. Avoiding Bertie's raised eyebrows, she carefully laid them out one by one on the table. Then finally she rasped that James had written a few brief letters to let them to let them know he was alright, but she hadn't found the courage yet to write back yet. She feebly tried to explain that she feared she would be tempting his fate by writing about the gentle life at home, whilst his life was in peril.

When Bertie asked why she hadn't told him about the letters, she answered by stating she didn't want him getting any glorified ideas of heroism. She wanted him to remain fearful of the wicked Hun and void of any courage or urges to fight them as he grew bigger and older. Sobbing relentlessly, she bemoaned that she had already lost a husband and a son and that she didn't want to lose another. Bertie did try to reassure, and hearten her by stressing James was not dead, and he himself had such no ambitions for firing a gun. Yet, he knew her heart was broken, and her mind was beyond considering anything other than tragedy. Only when James would finally return home would there be any hope that her spirits may be rekindled.

Sleep avoided them both that evening. Whist Bertie's ears hummed with the harrowing and relentless sobbing which leached through the bedroom walls, his mind willed the daylight so that he could finally write to his brother.

At least come the new dawn, he was happy there were no more secrets.

Chapter 13

He'd written to James several times, and with Millie's help, they sent two parcels containing the cigarettes and chocolates he requested, and in preparation for the arrival of the approaching winter, they dispatched several pairs of socks, woollen gloves and scarfs. Every day since the cheese hunt, he'd asked if the post boy had been, but as yet disappointedly she said James had not replied, and he believed her.

On the evening which would haunt him forever, he'd run home with excited leaps. His uncontrollable enthusiasm had arisen because Newt had stumbled upon an undamaged crate of Portuguese brandy and with one gripped in each hand all the gang had raced and skipped home in the nearing darkness to gift their spoils, and provide some much needed joy to their needy loved ones who were now beginning to suffer from the lack of any luxuries.

Bertie banged the two bottles down next to the letter which was entitled 'Royal Artillery War Dog Training School'

Glancing up from the simmering broth she was stirring, Bertie's Ma saw his face crease and his eyes flood with water. "I know it will be hard at first, but we all have to do out bit."

 "Do our bit!" His smile had vanished, replaced with an overbearing sense of dread which had welled up inside him. "Do our bit! Aren't we doing enough already?"

"Everyone has to do a little more." She raised the ladle to her mouth and sipped from the edge of the caldron.

"More! How much more can we do?" A shrill in his throat caused him to press his Adam's apple. "You help out in the sewing club. I keep a lookout for invaders and our James …. Our bloody James is knee deep in mud ducking from bloody deathly bullets."

"Bertie!"

He lifted the letter and through blurry eyes he scanned the first paragraph, which thanked Mrs Lanyon for volunteering Finn for war dog service.

"Why? Ma Why?" He screwed the paper and threw it into the fire below the stove. "We don't need the money."

"The army needs all the help they can get ……. Remember Bertie, that's what you said. Your words." She pinched a few granules of salt between her fingers and dropped the measly portion into the pan. "And besides, we can't keep Finn any longer."

Hearing his name, Finn cocked one ear and tilted his head as though he was listening, then he gave a little whimper and rubbed up against Bertie's leg.

"What? Why? What do you mean, we can't keep him?"

"You read the news. All dogs must be destroyed due to food shortage." She quoted the latest headline.

"That's rubbish. It's just not true." He patted Finns back and looked down at him. "Don't you listen Finn." His tail swished on the floor.

"That's what the paper say. People are starving and can't afford to feed their animals. Dead dogs are being burned on pyres in London."

Again she tasted the supper and unknowingly nodding her head with satisfaction.

"Not here there are not. I know everybody's being careful, but there's still plenty of scraps around here for one dog."

"Maybe not yet, but it's coming. I've heard them talking about it in Trewin. He'll be safer in the army." She slid the bottle of brandy to the middle of the table out of the way, replaced them with two bowls and two spoons, and returned to the stove.

Bertie felt sick. He had to look away from her and at Finn, who tilting his head and twitching his ears seemed to be listening to every word. They said.

"Safer?"

Stirring the broth and without looking up, she stated. "They're faster runners, can get through the small holes in the barbwire. No-man's-land means nothing to them. He'll be well fed and very well looked after. You won't have to worry about him starving to death." She pursed her lips in deep concentration as she considered adding another pinch of salt.

"He's not going! He shouted.

"Using Retrievers is better than risking a man's life, isn't it?" She grabbed a cloth and wrapped it around the pot handle and, carefully swivelling at the waist, she turned towards the table.

"I don't care. They are not taking him. He's ours, and he lives here."

"He's a dog."

94

"He's not. He's part of part family. Pa brought him home for us….. to look after him and not to send him away to be slaughtered in something that's nothing to do with him."

"Think of the lives he's going to save." She poured out half the steaming broth into the two bowls and turned to drop the pan back onto the range.

"That's their choice. This isn't Finns war. He doesn't understand bullets and cannons."

"Bertie. You must stop all this silliness over a dog."

"All the fellas that have gone off fighting, God bless em. Well, they chose to go. Didn't they and Finn hasn't. It's not his choice. He doesn't understand." He stroked his floppy ears and rubbed the back of his neck just how he liked it and he pressed his head against Bertie, urging for more.

"The Lieutenant is coming to collect him and he is taking him on the train to Kings Cross. He'll be at the training school for a few weeks where he'll start to learn how to get used to hearing all the gunfire, then when he's ready and fully trained, he'll be sent overseas. "

 She pulled back two chairs. "Now eat." With a straight back, she sat at the table and tilted her bowl to make it easier to spoon out her food.

"I'm not hungry."

She dipped in her spoon and raising the broth to her lips, she touched the end of the spoon with her tongue. "Wish we had some pepper."

"I hate that Lieutenant, and I don't care for what he thinks."

"Bertie! That man's doing a fine job for the country. Show him a little respect." She swallowed. "And besides, not all men volunteered. Some have been called up. Think of it as him being called up. It will make you proud of him."

"No Ma. It's not happening." Bertie's mouth was suddenly dry, and it was difficult for him to speak. "I won't let it. He's not going."

"Stop all this ridiculous fuss. Stop it now." She banged down her spoon on the table. "I can't believe you're being so selfish about a dog. Think about what everyone else has given up." She slid his bowl towards his seat. "Now come here and eat your supper whilst it's hot

"I can't. Not now. I'm thinking about us, and I think that we've already given enough up. We're not giving up anything else. This isn't going to happen. I'm not going to let it." He lowered down to Finn, his eyes now red and sore, and he coaxed Finn to lie on the cold slabs next to him. He curled around him and wrapped his arm over his neck and kissed his snout, and then he ran his fingers through his fur and Finn snorted happily to himself. "No one is going to hurt you, boy. I promise. "Again he hugged Finn tight. "I'm not letting them take you away from here …… ever."

"You don't have a choice." Ignoring her son's pain and desperation, she coldly stated. "The Lieutenant is coming for him tomorrow."

Bertie jumped up and shook his head and with gulping sobs, he shouted. "I hate this war and I hate you!" Then he shouted Finn to follow him out of the room. Defying his Ma's calls for him to return at once, Bertie clattered up the stairs with Finn bounding closely beside him.

96

He leaped across his bedroom, heeling the door shut in the process, he dived onto the bed.

Thinking Bertie was playing some sort of game, Finn flicked his tail from side to side in puzzlement, and then he too leaped on the bed for Bertie to wrap his cuddling and hugging arms around him.

"They're not taking you my fur face. I won't let them." He squeezed tight his arms and buried his face into his golden shaggy fur.

"I promise." Thumping his tail on the bed as if he seemed to understand every word Bertie said to him, Finn groaned and stared at the bedroom door. He knew he shouldn't be upstairs and on the bed, and expecting a scolding at any moment, he looked towards the door and listened to the bellowing rants from downstairs.

Bertie pretended to be asleep when his Ma cracked open the bedroom door to peep through the small gap and waiting for her to reprimand Finn, and order him from the room he firmed his hug around the dog to reassure him all was well, and prevent him from moving.

Whilst he hoped his Ma had been tempted to taste the brandy, and mix enough of it with her medicine to make her sleep, when she bumped her way into her own bedroom without even trying to disturb or reprimand Finn he knew she had drank more than she should have.

He's listened to the mantle clock slowly chime twelve right through to four, and so he was up a full hour before his normal work time. It was still dark, and he could see nothing but pitch. He hadn't slept for a moment during the tediously long night, in which he did nothing but hug Finn, ruffle his fur, kiss him, and listen to him dreaming.

He silently dropped one foot out of the bed and rested his bare sole on the cold floor, then after listening to his Ma breathing beyond the door across the small hallway, he slid out of bed. Hushing Finn as he kissed his snout, he hauled him up in his arms, paused once more to listen to his Ma's noisy breathing, then hoping Finn's groan hadn't awoken her he crept out of the bedroom and down the stairs with soundless feet all the time hugging Finn tight to his chest.

Within minutes he had emerged into the cold brisk air of dawn's birdsong of the dying night with a satchel full rations swinging from his back and before the tweeting of dawn's birdsong he was running across the cliff top fields with his excited, but confused friend bounding by his side.

"Now you stay here boy." Bertie instructed Finn as he checked the strength of the rope and the knot. It was tight, but to double check, he wedged two more boulders on top of the fastening.

Looking directly at Bertie, Finn whined and shook his tail, then slanting his head, he playfully raised one paw for Bertie to shake.

"I know boy, but you're safe here." He knew Finn was confused. "No one will come down here." He wrapped his arms around his back of his neck and snuggled his face into Finn's fur.

Hiding a small piece of paper with his address under Finn's collar, he begged. "But you've got to be quiet."

Quintals Cave was extremely dark being only lit from the half moon's reflection on the sea, but Bertie knew it well enough to arrange the rope and rocks into a comfy bed whilst securing Finn to stop him from following him back up the narrow path out of Horseshoe Cove.

"It won't be for long."

Tears sprang from his eyes and flowed down his face as he filled Finn's bowl with water and placed around it his favourite chewing toy, an old marrow bone and several small heaps of dried meat and fish.

"It's just until I finish work."

Finn's eyebrows raised and his tail wagged when he saw and smelt his breakfast.

"Then I'll come and get you."

Rising from his knees, he rubbed Finn's forehead. "I promise."

He didn't want to stop rubbing, and he didn't want to leave him. He couldn't bear the thought of leaving him alone in the cave, and he'd only walked a few steps before he was compelled to turn back and return to touch Finn again.

"Everything will be ok." He stroked Finn's face and kissed his snout several times in quick succession. "You just stay here and be quiet. Please, please, please Finn, please be quiet. Be very quiet."

The dog whimpered as Bertie tearfully reached the exit of the cave and this time reluctantly, but feeling it necessary, raised his voice a little and pointed his finger back into the darkness.

"Finn, stay boy. Be a good boy and be quiet."

He knew Finn was obedient, and that he would obey, but he also knew he would be wondering why he had been left there when he had done nothing wrong.

He hated himself for leaving him alone in the damp cave and his leg trembled and he felt sick, but drawing in a long breath he whispered.

"It's only until he finished work boy..... I'll soon be back...... I promise."

Then wiping away the tears from his cheeks, he ran up the narrow snaking path to the cliff tops, where he paused and listened. He stared across the misty fields towards the hazy village.

All was still peaceful and quiet, the early morning dullness not yet intruded by the igniting of lanterns by the early risers who would also soon be on their way to work.

Finally, after being sure no one had seen him, and only being able to hear the rolling of the waves crash in the cove below, he lowered his head and ran away from the cliff top to occupy himself with work all the time hoping Old Man Corney would let him finish early knowing that he had got in and started before the others arrived.

Chapter 14

"No! No! No!" Bertie's screams echoed all around Quintal's Cave and out beyond the fields above Horseshoe Cove.

"Finn?" He picked up the rope, and through blurry eyes, he looked around the cave. Finn had eaten his food, but his toy, bone and dish, still half full of water, was all where Bertie had left them. He picked up the rope and held it at arm's length. It had not been chewed.

The day had dragged slowly by until now. All day long Bertie couldn't stop thinking about Finn, alone in Quintal's Cave. He hoped and prayed he'd be quiet, no barking, just eat, play and go to sleep. Old Man Corney hadn't eased his worries any, he'd been as mean as ever and not allowed Bertie to finish a few minutes earlier, even though he'd started over an hour before normal work time and worked through all his duties without a break . He now despised the silver-haired weaselly man.

"No Finn, please God no." He dropped to his knees and cried, then angrily he threw away the rope and ran as fast as he could up the winding path, and across the cliff tops toward home. Sweat of fear dampened his brow and dried his throat.

"It's no use blubbering or shouting. He's gone." His Ma was waiting for him as he barged through the kitchen door.

"No! No! No!"

Bertie swayed through a spasm of weakness and his legs disobeyed him. He dropped to his knees, his back closing the door as he banged against it and slumped to the floor, destroyed.

"9 o'clock train from Trewin, as planned." Conscience free of any guilt and concerns, she remained sat in her chair, staring into the small fire of the range.

"No Ma, no. How could you?" Drawing his knees up to his chest, he dropped his head into his hands and cried despairingly.

"You know why." She didn't break her glare from the faint yellow flickers or display any sympathy for her son's agony. "We went over all that last night. No point in doing it all again."

"No, I can't believe you'd do this." He shook his head and tears dropped to the slabs. "Not to Finn. Not to us. How could you?"

"It's for the best."

"How could you be so mean and cruel?"

"I had no option. Things are going to get real tough soon. Besides, you knew they'd come for him eventually. Either to take him away or ….."

"No, no. Not our poor Finn." Bertie could hardly speak. "He loves us."

"I've told you, he will be better off." She leant forward and, grabbing the poker, she prodded the edges to flick over the grey ash into the glowing centre of the fire. "They'll look after him."

"He'll be wondering what's happening to him. He's never been anywhere without us, let alone on a train……….Where is he?"

"He's safe. That's all you need to know."

"How do you mean? All I need to know."

"You're not going to find him."

He now regretted throwing into the fire the details of the Dogs Corps. He cussed his haste and anger. He could have kept the address and run away to save Finn from the bullets of the Hun.

"I can't believe this is happening. I can't believe what you've done."

She didn't reply. Her face remained dispassionate.

"I can't bear thinking about him being alone."

She refused to look away from the fire.

"How did you know?" He tried to wipe clear the water from his eyes with his knuckles, but they immediately welled and water ran down his cheeks again.

"Know?"

"Yes. Know where he was." He stammered.

"Mother's intuition."

"Mother! A mother wouldn't have done this. A mother wouldn't be that cruel. That's why James left, not because of the war, because of you being so cruel." He spat.

"Bertie. You don't mean that. You're just upset."

"Yes I do. You're mean and I hate you. Hate you! You hear me? I hate you!"

He sprang to his feet and pulled back the door. He didn't hear her shout, "What about your supper?"

In that moment, he didn't want to hear or see her ever again. He didn't regret his outburst and he meant every word of it. With tears blinding him and memories of Finn flashing before him, he ran and stumbled across the cliff tops toward Horseshoe Cove screaming out Finn's name over and over again.

Chapter 15

Although it would be another hour before the night sky darkened the village, the five of them gathered around the corner lamppost, the traditional meeting point for the yearly South Cliff conker contest. A date, and a contest that was no longer considered a worthy enough event to underline on the kitchen calendars.

Long since faded in the memory, mainly due to the relocating of the village folk, was the enthusiasm for smashing conker's or knuckles for the reward of gulping down a free drink of their choice from the now derelict ale house, whilst having the pleasure of watching, to cheers and pats on the back, the losing finalist carving deep the winners initials in the huge horse chestnut tree which spread it mammoth twisting branches high and wide to shadow the lamppost.

No longer did the interested extend beyond anyone, but Bertie, Drake, Millie, Lily and Newt. Curtains and tattered nets briefly jerked, only to hang still once again as the fleeting interest of the observers, who had been slightly intrigued and confused by the small gathering, quickly waned.

It was Newt's idea to continue with the contest, he had mentioned it to Millie and Lily a few days earlier, and they agreed to rekindle the interest of the older boys, hoping the fun would ease Bertie's pain and momentarily distract him from tormenting himself about Finn.

All five of them looked up at the bark scarred with the carvings of long gone, but never to be forgotten winners. Bertie briefly smiled at seeing James's initials brightly dominating the rest of the carvings.

"Do you think James will have organised a competition amongst the soldiers?" Newt stuttered, fondly remembering how he made it to last year's final, only to be beaten by Bertie's brother.

"Probably." Bertie proudly smiled. "He won't like sitting around just playing cards and telling tales." Recalling his enthusiasm for organizing fun. "He'll probably get them up and keep em busy playing football if it's far enough away from the bullets of the sneaky Hun. If not, he'll smash them all at marbles."

"I would have had a good chance of winning this year, if I'd have been able to find another conker like last year's beauty." Newt smiled as he recalled his dad pickling it for him, soaking it in vinegar and then baking it without the others knowing.

"Doubt it, you were just lucky." Drake scoffed, practising his swing. "Besides, it was the size of a small coconut, and there hasn't been any that big this year."

"It was a six-er. That would probably be enough to win it this year." He still hoped to get his initials engraved on the tree.

"Nobody got anything to challenge this then." Bertie held up, by it's string, the dark and wizened champion of last year.

"No way." Newt gasped.

"You saved it?" Millie smiled.

"Found it in our James's draw." Bertie smiled. "The champion and record holding nine-er."

"It won't make to be a 10-er." Drake blustered.

A Boy, a Dog and the Great War

"Same rules?" Bertie ignored him.

"Same rules." Drake repeated with a grin. "Three conkers each, three swings per battle. We all play each other until there is only one of us left."

"Who's doing the draw?" Bertie asked, looking in the direction of the girls.

"Can I do it?" Lily's hand darted into the air. "Please let me do it I've brought a piece of coal."

"Alright then." Millie sanctioned. "I'll collect the stones."

Millie quickly collected five stones, and held them out for Lily to take and scratch their initials on the back with the coal, then she shook the stones in her cupped hands, and one by one, slowly and deliberately she dropped them to the floor.

"Drake." They all called together as the first stone thudded into the mud. "Versus Lily." The girls gasped, and the boy's grinned when the letter L rolled to a stop next to it the D.

"Bertie verses Millie." They confirmed as the B thudded next to the M.

"Newt to fight me." Drake boasted.

"Or me." Lily corrected. "He goes up against the winner."

"That's what I said. He fights me." He ruffled her hair to increase her agitation then commanded. "Ok, show em. Hold em up."

The boys shuffled their fingers inside their pockets and the girls delicately opened their knitted purses until together they held out in front of them their selected and prepared firepower. After quickly flicking their eyes along the line of shoe laced dangling conker's, and holding them side by side to compare and ensure the strings were all the same length, they stepped aside to allow Drake and Lily to take up the correct stance.

"Ladies first." Bertie suggested as Lily and Drake stood a yard apart, facing each other.

"My letter dropped first." Drake argued, flexing the conker on the shoelace.

"I don't mind." Lily yielded, outstretching her arm and standing in front of Drake as she wrapped the shoelace around her knuckles to prevent her conker from being knocked out of her grasp.

"Miss." The gang laughed, and hailed in together as Drake's wild swing made contact with nothing but air, and losing his balance, he fell face forward into the dirt.

"Just warming up." He quickly retorts, re-adjusting his clothing with an angry frown. Then, determined to prove to them he was right, his next swing struck Lily's conker on the full, splitting it into two pieces to make it the first casualty in the competition.

"Here we go" He grinned as his third swing found its target perfectly, and shattered with ease her second conker. In return, none of Lily's tame swings were powerful enough to inflict any damage on Drake's two-er, and stuffing his prized weapon of destruction into his pocket he stood aside boasting a huge satisfied grin.

108

Bertie and Millie were next to take the stand, and it soon became obvious to all around that Bertie did not exert enough effort into his attacks to make a score, and after the six strikes had been completed both of them still had their three conker's intact.

"No scores." Drake huffed.

Eager to enter the fray next, Newt lined up next to face off against Drake, but he soon found himself out of the competition without even making a strike as Drake's first two swings obliterated his conker's and the third attack smashed against his hand so hard it split open his knuckle.

"I'm out." Newt winced quickly clamping his left hand on top of his swelling right knuckle.

"Out?" Millie rushed to his side. "Let me take a look." But embarrassed, and squinting to fend off tears, Newt dropped his remaining conker, turned his shoulder to dejectedly trudged away and slump his back against the ancient tree.

Now with four of them left, Lily sullenly kicked away Newt's stone. "Second round." She sighed as she gathered up the remaining stones to drop them slowly once more, one by one.

"Bertie verses Drake. Millie against me." She shouted over to Newt, who rubbing his swollen and bleeding skin, wondered how a little conker could inflict so much pain.

Without hesitation, the oldest two boys adjusted their feet to face each other.

"Drake to go first." Lily needlessly announced because everyone knew it was the privilege of the competition's leader to strike first.

"Are you using James's champion?" Drake urged.

"No." Bertie replied, squeezing his two substitutes between his fingers. "Saving it for the final." He finished his selection.

"Makes no difference." Drake pulled back to shoulder height his conker and swung. 'Whack' his first swing smashed Bertie's into several flying pieces.

"You'll not be reaching the final." He grinned.

Bertie frowned, looked at his dangled string, and shook his head. He was dismayed by how effortlessly Drake had exercised destruction.

"Five-er." Drake cheered, clutching his victorious conker in his hand and stretching his arm above his head in triumph. "This is going all the way."

Bertie fiddled in his pocket and pulled out his second best. His eyes fixed on Drake's smug face as he held out firm and level his arm.

Drake nodded and confidently shouted. "Super chopper swing." And then he rapidly swung his conker holding arm, flailing it rapidly in a continuous circle motion, whoosh, whoosh, whoosh until he smashed his missile perfectly against its defenceless target. Pieces of nut flew in all directions, and Bertie once again was left holding an empty boot lace.

"Yes! Get in there, you beauty" Drake clenched his fist around his conker and punched the air to celebrate again. "Six-er and still going strong."

"Been practising." Bertie wiped a piece of glossy brown from his brow.

"Might as well start carving my initials up now, Millie." He whooped in her face, but folding her arms across her chest, she quickly turned her head away, displaying her disapproval of his gloating.

"A gent wins with dignity." She whispered to herself.

"What?" Drake laughed.

"Nothing." She walked away.

"Last one Bertie." Drake turned back to face his opponent. "Get it out. Get out the nine-er for the last time."

Bertie stared at the wizened dark seed in his palm. He sighed, clutching it tight, and for the briefest of moments, and hoping no one had seen him, he closed his eyes and tilted his head to the sky. 'Please God.'

"Stop your time wasting Bertie. It's time. My champion verses yours …. No mercy. No prisoners."

Bertie wet his finger and dampened James's conker, and then he shined it on his hip before holding it out disconsolately for Drake's to attack.

"Drum roll, please." Drake turned his head sideways again, and flicked his eyes across the displeased faces of Newt, Millie and Lilly, however ignoring him, they hoped his conqueror had weakened from all the vicious attacks.

"Strings!" Bertie was the first to react as Drake's aim had been ill judged and clipping the edge of James's conker, both his and Bertie's laces had become entwined in a spinning coil.

"My turn." Bertie gasped and he unintentionally allowed Drake to untangle, and pull apart both the conkers.

"Give it your best Bertie." Millie hoped out loud as she watched Drake toss back to Bertie, James's champion conker.

"Now here we go." Bertie returned the faintest of smiles to Millie. "For James."

He drew in a large breath, and then, without delay, leaped high to thrust down on Drake's conker with an almighty smash. The contact thud sounded perfect, and Drake's conker spun over his knuckles. However, it was the two chunks of last year's winner that flew into the air.

"Yes! Yes! Yes! Seven-er." Drake whacked his clenched fist against his thigh and then arrogantly thrust it into the air again. "What did I tell you Bertie?" He stretched out his neck and leaned forward. "There's no stopping me now."

He gloated so close to Bertie's face that Bertie saw his reflection in Drake's triumphant eyes.

Millie stepped up behind Bertie and patted him on his shoulder. He turned away, defeated and struggling to ignore Drake's humiliating taunts and the awkwardness caused by his bragging.

"Who's next for the slaughter?" Drake shouted, his eyes triumphantly wide and his feet excitedly tapping the cobbles as though he were standing on hot coals.

"Wait your turn." Lily said, holding up her hand with judging authority.

112

"It's mine and Millie's turn to go now. You go up against the winner."

However, it was clear to all that both Lily and Millie had lost their enthusiasm for playing. Fearing to meet Drake in the final, when they finally stepped up and took it in turns to guide only effortless and timid swings at each other the contest was only decided because Lily's remaining conker was already weak and on it's third swing it split without making any contact and dropped to the floor.

"Me and Millie in the final." Drake wasted no time knowing his victory was assured. "Millie and me." He grinned directly into her eyes. "Come on, Millie."

"I've had enough." She began to turn away.

"No, you can't." Drake reached out to drop his hand on her shoulder. "It's tradition."

"No Millie, no." Newt, still rubbing his knuckles, stretched his neck up from his injury to look in her direction.

"Millie?" Lily moaned, slanting her head.

Millie shook her head and shrugged off Drake's detaining hand. She looked at Bertie for help.

After looking at Newt's, and Lily's, disconsolate faces, he shrugged. "We ought to finish it. It's only right."

Drake had no intention of taking it easy or trying to impress Millie with any unusual gentlemanly conduct. As leader of the contest, he was entitled to go first, and so without guilt he went on the attack first with both his first shots, shattering Millie's conker's into flying fragments.

"Eight-er!" Not relenting from his vicious and powerful attacks, and not compromising his force to allow her at least one strike in the final, he strutted forward and angled himself sidewards to swing up his right leg high before launching into a twisting jump to increase the speed of contact.

"Sidewinder" Newt gasped loudly, but Drake's foot splattered in the mud his conker missed it's target and wrapped around Millie's lace only to then snap free from his hand and roll across the cobbles stopping only when it collided into Bertie's boot.

Drake held his breath as he watched Bertie arch over and reach down to grab the rolling champion.

"What?" Bertie frowned as he straightened with the conker in his hand. "What in the hell?" He held up the lace and dangled the conker in front of him to bewildering gazes.

"What's going on Drake?" Bertie yelled, pulling from his back pocket a small folding knife.

"Bertie?" Millie scowled. "What is it?" Her eyes gaped and her jaw hung slack.

"What's wrong?" Lily gasped.

Drake opened his mouth, but he couldn't speak. His face paled, and every fearing muscle locked rigid. His throat became dry and his cheeks flustered red. Bertie straightened out his knife blade and scraped it against the side of the conker to peel off a small sliver of dark brown paint from the surface of an iron round ball.

"You cheat!" He shouted. "You lousy, no good cheat."

Millie and Lily immediately surrounded Bertie to inspect his findings and Newt stopped inspecting his damaged knuckle and rose up from his knees to see what the fuss was all about.

"Arr. Just a bit of fun, that's all." Drake feigned a smile and turned over his palms with a gesture to support his innocence.

"Drake?" Millie flashed an astounded glance in his direction. "How could you?"

"I was going to tell you." He muttered. "I swear ……. I was."

"Really?" Millie shook her head. "I can't believe you'd cheat on us…..Your friends."

"Oh Millie, come on. Can't you take a joke? It was just a bit of fun." His eyes flicked across their accusing faces, which were now gathered around the fake conker.

"You were never going to tell us." Newt scowled, now understanding why he had a huge bloodied lump on his knuckles.

"Oh come on Newt. Of course I was." He laughed. "Listen to you to you all. What's wrong with you? Where's your sparkle gone?" His forehead glistened with sweat beads of humiliation.

"Sparkle?" Bertie held up his hand with the steel ball displayed between his finger and thumb. "This is no joke, Drake."

 "It was just a bit of fun."

"But it isn't. Is it Drake?" Millie grabbed Newt's injured hand and held it up. "This is not funny."

"Ah you're just a bunch of sore losers." He kicked away the coal initialled pebbles and turned his back. "Who cares anyway? It's just a silly game for kids." He shouted over his shoulder.

"I've waited all year for this!" Newt stuttered.

"Then you're a f f f f fool, Newt." Drake ridiculed Newt by mimicking him.

"And you're a cheat and a liar." Newt forced a shout without a stammer.

Drake stopped. "And?" He spun to face the gang. The crimson flush in his cheeks replaced with paleness. "What are you going to do about it, eh? Come on Newt, you dumb little pipsqueak." He sucked in air to expand his chest with the threat. "What you going to do about it?" He saw Newt flick his eyes up to Bertie for support. "Or you Bertie" It wasn't a question, it was a challenge, and he clenched his fists. "Think you can do something about it?" He tilted his head arrogantly and sneered. "Drop the knife and fight like a man." He raised his fists and firmed his feet in the dirt. "Show the girls how good you are at everything." Then he winked at Millie. "Well, let's see how good you are without your James protecting you."

Bertie threw the ball as hard as he could at Drake, but without too much effort Drake shot out his hand and caught the ball with ease.

"Is that the best you can do?" Grinning, he clenched the iron ball in his right hand.

"You cheated, and you smashed our James's conker." Bertie rolled up his sleeves and equalled Drake's fighting stance.

"Aww" Drake mocked.

"You're not one of us anymore." Bertie took one purposeful stride forward.

"Us?" Drake equalled the advance.

"Yes us. The TVC's."

Drake laughed. "Oh that. Don't you mean the TVCC's?" He laughed "Trewin's Voluntary Children's Corps. Well, you know something Bertie Lanyon. You're right, I'm not and come the summer I'm off to get a real gun and do some proper fighting against the Huns." He imitated firing a rifle at Bertie. "Not waste my time pretending to be a toy soldier in a crockery wooden den with a bunch of little children." His narrowed eyes flashed a glance of hate across the startled and hurt faces of the rest of the gang.

"Stop this. Both of you. Stop it at once." Millie leaped between them and held out both of her hands as a barrier. "Now, like you said, Drake. It was just a bit of fun, so stop this nonsense at once."

Both the boys ignored her plea and continued to walk slowly towards each other. Both Lily's and Newt's legs trembled and their feet refused to move.

They hated the idea of their friends trying to hurt each other and, although they shouted for them to stop, they were too afraid to step any closer.

117

"Bertie! Listen to me!" Millie screamed, but he barged passed her to move within striking distance of Drake's grin. "It was only meant to be a bit of fun." She shouted into his ear, then without any indecision from behind, she leaped up to wrap her arms tight around his chest and clamp his arms by his side. "Don't do it. Don't let him upset you. He's not worth it."

No one was really surprised when he allowed Millie to hold him from advancing and engaging Drake with swinging fists. Everyone knew he could easily shrug away her restraints, but they all wondered if he could really hit his friend and inflict pain on the boy he'd grown up with, no matter how angered and betrayed he felt.

Drake sensed his hesitation. "That's right, listen to the girls and run away, just like you always do." He harboured no such doubts. He had no regard for sentiments and he was prepared to hurt his friend if he had to.

Bertie shook his head, and then finally turned away, reluctantly ignoring Drake's attempts to embarrass him. Allowing Millie's hand to lead him within, he knew Drake was right about them playing war. The belittling had hurt him, but he also knew the argument had simply increased the inevitable, the final days of the TVC.

"Go and run to the shanty you call the Command Centre or better still go and hide yourself in Quintal's Cave."

Bertie halted to twist back his head to blaze a bemused glare towards Drake and, as he did so, Mille stumbled.

118

"What?" He yelled. Something about hiding in Quintal's Cave irked him.

"You heard me. Run away." Drake laughed. "Run away to your hiding place with your little sea urchins."

Confused by Drake's laughing taunt, Bertie began to turn towards Drake once more, but as he did so Lily linked his other arm and Newt dashed by their side to help Millie steady herself.

Together the three of them continued to guide Bertie towards the dewy cliff top grass and away from the bully, who continued with his gloating taunts as they disappeared in the evening dusky distance.

Chapter 16

22nd October

Mrs Lanyon

In reply to your request dated 20th September.

Your son James Lanyon is assigned to my command, and therefore, I know him well. He is an excellent infantry man, much liked by the men, and highly efficient at all duties assigned to him.

May I say that I am astonished to learn that he is much under the regulation age as he is very tall and well developed. In addition, James looks much older than many of my men, and he is naturally stronger and considerably bolder.

As you well understand, we are considerably under constant pressure over here, and so consequently I am disinclined to send such a useful soldier back home upon the request of his mother.

I have discussed James's age issue with my superiors, and in line with my opinions, they too are reluctant to loose such a good man due to the negative consequences, one of which includes the demoralisation of the other soldiers.

In addition, we agreed that we do not feel it necessary to dismiss him as under age when he is physically superior to those serving here alongside him. For that reason, our rule is, if the boy is up to the tasks which lay ahead, he should stay irrespective to his age.

May I take this opportunity to add, you will be pleased to know that James is a great credit to you and your family in these dire times and I am proud to lead forth the troops of the King towards our adversary's line with such a courageous and stalwart soldier behind me.

Yours Sincerely

T A Bridges Lt Col

5th Battalion Duke of Cornwall's Light Infantry.

He didn't wait until his Ma left the home to read the letters now. He didn't care if he hurt her feelings or disobeyed her. She had fractured his carefree nature and destroyed his considerations, and apart from yearning for Finn, he was emotionless. Even when James left, he did not feel this much pain. He could not remember feeling this much agony before Finn had been betrayed.

The small two-roomed cottage no longer felt like home. It had felt strange when James left, but now without Finn there was no longer any warmth and love. It was a spiritless stone and brick shell, suitable only for providing cover from the oncoming of the bracing winter.

Losing Finn choked him beyond participating in any banter and child's play, and now his presence in the Command Centre was noted only by his sullenness and lack of motivation.

His unbearable silences and the conker incident had stifled the gang's enthusiasm for conducting their duties, and no longer did they rush out from the comfort of their homes to shiver in the dampness of the Command Centre.

Seeing Bertie behave this way hurt Millie. She sympathised for his loss, and resolutely, with Lily's help, she tried to keep the gang's friendship together by organizing the lookout duties and treasure rummaging timetables.

Carefully, the girls tentatively and tactfully tried their best to rally him into taking part, but reddy eyed and completely uninterested, he just slumped in the corner with his head sagging to the floor. He now rarely purchased to read out 'The War Illustrated' and no longer did he spurn the gang into action with his rousing gusto. He was lost in a world of grief and it was obvious to all around him he was only there because he didn't want to be at home with his Ma.

He went to work before she had risen and he stayed out until she had extinguished of the kitchen lantern. Mostly he was slouched in the corner of the Command Centre, but generally he didn't care if he had to stay out for hours in the cold and rain waiting for the death of the kitchen light.

She had tried to reason with him, many times, but on each occasion he raged with a fury born from her treachery. He could not forget Finn, and he would never forgive her. His heart was pained and his soul was empty.

Millie took it upon herself to feed him, sneaking out her half eaten meals and scraps of left-overs as her unaware parents were busily occupied doing what every normal family did at meal times, talk about the war and the daily casualty listings. Now everyone in South Cliff knew someone who had been affected by the Great War, the war which the experts promised would be over by Christmas.

Still, she'd tried to cheer him up with apple pie and cream, it roused him enough to lick the plate, but the real turning point came when Millie deliberately compared him to his Ma, at first angered he stormed out from the Command Centre, but the following day after contemplating her observations, and listening to her heartfelt concerns he began to slowly display indications of the old Bertie which she welcomingly recognised.

However, it wasn't only Bertie who had been quiet throughout the passing of autumn. Having still not received any news about his father, Newt's stammer had worsened so much that he now had to pause and draw breath every time he spoke, and when he did, he could not prevent himself from uncontrollably repeating the first letter of every sentence eight times. Everyone finally now understood his condition was as a result of the worrying and they ignored his handicap the best they could. Even Drake, who rarely attended their gatherings, had stopped calling him demeaning names and teasing him.

With the onset of the cold dull days and early evening darkness, he too had begun acting strangely aloof. He was now totally unreliable, disinterested, and he kept himself at a distance most of the time. Mainly he was only interested in gathering washed up wood for the village stoves and searching for bottles of alcohol.

As they walked home on the bitterly cold and perfectly cloud free night Millie, whispering so that Newt, Lily and Drake, who were all several faces ahead, admitted to Bertie that keeping a look out the Germans, and searching for treasure no longer seemed like fun, and she worried the approaching stormy winter could bring an end to the gang's activities for good.

Bertie did little to ease her apprehension, murmuring back maybe they were all just getting older, and they were now out growing the childish games, and besides without Finn it was no longer the same. Regretfully, Millie agreed, but with little else to keep them occupied in the near abandoned village, she vowed she would do her best to find something interesting to keep the gang together. Pulling out a letter from his back pocket and unfolding it to the shimmer of the moon he told her, that her intentions were soon to get a whole lot more difficult.

29th October

Dear Ma & Bertie

There is no kind way to say this, so I will just tell you straight. Whilst we were on the banks of the prettiest valley, you could ever see we were unexpectedly engaged by heavy bombardment and an absolute hail of machine gun fire.

Unfortunately for me, a jagged piece of shrapnel lodged itself into my shoulder and after the Hun's devastation had eased I was ordered to report to the field hospital in Vimy where I had an unpleasant and unfortunate encounter with Billy 'Newt' Newton from No 4.

The poor fellow has taken a direct hit to his face, which has destroyed half of his face and taken both of his eyes. Although his lungs still function perfectly well, he can't walk, talk or move in any way. The poor chap is as good as dead, and if God had shown any mercy, he would be.

No doubt, if she hasn't already, the pitiable Missus Newton will receive a letter from his captain very soon. Be prepared.

James.

"Oh, dear God no!" Millie held her hand over her mouth to contain her anguish, but her gasped caused the three darkened figures ahead to pause from their stride and turn.

Bertie scrunched the paper in his hand to hide it from view.

"Think I stood on a slug." Said Millie and unconcerned her friends returned to their own chatter.

"What should we do?" She returned her hand to her mouth and whispered.

"What can we do?" Bertie shrugged woefully as he looked at Newt's silhouette displaying a rare moment of joy with Lily.

"Maybe he will get better." 'Please God' Millie momentarily closed her eyes.

"Doesn't sound like it." Bertie saw her tilt her head back to the stars.

"Newt will just be glad he's coming home." Tears glistened as they rolled down her cheek.

Chapter 17

"Oh poor Miss Cavell. She was only doing her job as a nurse." Millie's fingers stretched out in the dark to grab Bertie's hand. Again, and as usual now there'd been just the two of them on duty in the Command Centre, and as normal with nothing to see, but the shimmer of the moon and stars on the black sea they'd securitized every report from the latest edition of 'The War Illustrated'. Millie was relieved Bertie had begun to show an interest in the war again.

When the yellow tinge from their last candle faded out and their shivers could not be controlled, they despondently trudged over the white crisp cliff top and back toward the ice twinkling village.

Millie didn't need Bertie's hand to guide her along the way in the darkness. She needed to feel his closeness, and she yearned for a moment's tenderness after reading the distressing news about the tragic nurse.

"They don't care." He replied being oblivious to her yearning. "They are simply evil."

"To execute the poor women like that." She clasped his hand, but there was no reciprocation. "It must have been terrible for her. I hope she managed to stay courageous right until the end." She held the squeeze. "Show the cowards what us Brits are made of." She imagined the heroine holding her head up high as the Germans secured the blind fold.

"I bet she did. War is for the brave and the devil Hun cowards are cruel." Bertie released the hold.

"Our James says even though they look normal enough, they're all devils without the horns."

They neared the idle lamppost, and stepping away from Millie, Bertie turned to face home. He stared along the bleak row of cottages opposite, his eyes loitering on the middle house, his mind wondering if Newt had understood the severity of his Pa's injuries.

"Spawn of the devil, my Pa calls them." Millie wrapped her arms around her body and rubbed her sides as her shivers grew.

"One of us is going to have to go and find out." Bertie declared. "My Ma won't leave the house again."

Instinctively, Millie understood. "If Lily's rid herself of the sniffles, I'll get her to call in with me tomorrow." She too, stared at Newt's unlit home. "Hope that we can get him to come back with us to the Command Centre."

She returned to face Bertie, but his darkened figure was already disappearing into the blackness. "Oh." She dejectedly gasped. "See you tomorrow?" She wished loudly.

"Same time." She could just make out his hand waving as he answered.

The lifting of the door latch did not raise his Ma from her slumber in the fireside chair. On her lap was one page of a letter, on the floor discarded at her feet was another, and in her hand was an empty black bottle. Immediately his eyes gaped at the large bold heading 'Royal Artillery War Dog School' and without disturbing his Ma he lifted the letter from her lap and angled it toward the candle.

127

30th December

Dear Mr Bertie Lanyon

In normal circumstances, I do not normally write to the owners of dogs, however on this occasion, due to finding the forwarding address hidden under Finn's collar, I decided to go against my normal principles and our rules. I would, first of all, like to take this opportunity to thank you for volunteering such a wonderful specimen of breed for the war effort. Finn has adapted outstandingly well, and he gets along with all our handlers and dogs equally delightfully. He has successfully been trained to return to his kennel from a distance of four miles from a previously unknown point of origin, and in addition to his tracking skills he has now become fully accustomed to the sound of gun fire and cannon blast. I am delighted to inform you, so positive has been his training that tomorrow morning he will be deployed to a sectional kennel in Northern France, and sometime shortly afterwards he will be allocated to his specific unit on the front line where he will deliver messages between the outposts and the gun batteries.

I am sure my news will make you extremely proud.

Yours Sincerely

S M Brackenridge - Special Dog Handling Lieutenant

Royal Artillery War Dog Training School

With tears rolling down his face, he looked at the address and the date. Eight days ago, he then picked up the other sheet and swapped the letters in his hand.

December 8th 1916

Dear Ma & Bertie,

Snow, snow, snow, snow. It's not stopped here for days on end now and it's very strange to see the charming ground ahead of us which seems so clean and heavenly with it's extreme whiteness, and yet we all know it is full of the dead and dying. It's horribly cold, of course, and as usual, the slush and mud in our trench is awful.

Unable to think of nothing except Finn in the freezing battle field Bertie threw the letters into his Ma's lap and ran to the tin bowl to heave and retch.

"Bertie?"

His clumsiness jolted her from her nap and being startled, the letters slid on her lap.

"I hope you're happy." He spat with a mouthful of bile.

Still drowsy and disoriented, she instinctively reached to grab the papers. "I told you he'd be well looked after." She slurred, trying in vain to hold up her head. Then she scrunched the letters in her palm as she tried to prevent them from falling to the floor. Once the letters were within her grasp, she sighed and her head began to drop forwards.

Her eyes lids fluttered and without being fully roused, she once more began to succumb to the effects of the relaxant. "If it wasn't for your friend." She mumbled, falling back to sleep.

"Friend?" Bertie pulled his head up from the tin bowl and swilled his mouth out with the stale water from the jug. "Friend?" He spat whilst spinning to her side.

She muttered something inaudible and exhaled only a snoring hiss.

"Friend?"

Bertie shook her by the shoulder and her head rocked from side to side and the letter fluttered to the floor. He shook her again, and she moaned, but without opening her eyes, she muttered. "Yes, the nice polite one." She yawned. "If it wasn't for him, Finn would have been put to sleep by now."

He bent his knees and lowered his ear next to her face. "Ma……. Friend….. Ma……… Which one?"

"I've told you." Her words were shallow and faint.

He shook her again, this time with forcefulness and again she whispered. "The one I met when I was out looking for him."

"Finn?"

"Yes Finn. I knew you'd hidden him somewhere. "Her lips barely parted. "And your friend said I should try Quintal's Cave."

"Which friend Ma? Which one?"

"I've told you. The nice mannered young man. I told him I couldn't possibly go down there so he offered to go for me, and a few minutes later he was on our doorstep with Finn."

"Who was Ma?" Who was it?"

"Hammit's lad. From round the corner."

"Drake! Damn it. It was Drake who found Finn." "Yes. Young Hammit.....
Drake Hammit ...... The nice young fella."

Bertie didn't hear her final words as she drifted away praising the boy
for his helpfulness because an all dictating rage had consumed his
judgement.

Slamming the door so hard a waft of air flickered the flame from the
lantern, Bertie hurled the rear yard gate and sped down the back alley,
only stopping when he skidded in the frost to a halt outside Drake's
bedroom window. He picked up a hand full of dirt and picked out
several small stones, which he then threw one by one at Drake's
window until eventually a bewildered Drake slid up the sash.

"Get out here!"

"Bertie?" Drake angled his head out of the window, yawned, stretched,
and squinted out into the darkness. "What's?" He shook the drowsiness
from his head and rubbed his slitty eyes to ensure he wasn't dreaming.
"What's going on? What do you want?"

"Get out here!" Bertie shouted, not caring whose sleep he disturbed.

"What time is it?" Drake replied faintly.

"Who cares? Just get out here. And now."

"What for?"

"Oh, you know what for." Bertie menaced.

"But it's freezing." Drake vigorously rubbed his body with his hand as he hesitated.

"I don't care. Get down here now."

"No! Go away."

"I'm going nowhere until you come down here."

"I'm not coming out, so home. I'm going back to bed."

"Get out here!" Bertie did not feel the freezing mizzle that glistened hazy in the air and shone on the walls and trees about him.

"No, it's late." He reached up to pull down the sash and close the window. "Whatever it is, it can wait until tomorrow."

"I'm warning you, Drake!" Bertie felt along the ground to find a larger stone. "Get out here now or the next stones coming straight through the glass." Then he pulled back his arm.

"Idiot. You're a brainless idiot Bertie Lanyon." The window slammed closed and Drake's ghostly face disappeared until just moments later the back door screeched open and Drake, wearing only a vest and his night time leggings, paced out.

"Right, I'm here, so what do you want?" His tone displayed impatience.

"You know why I'm here."

Bertie pushed open the small wooden gate and stepped inside the narrow cobbled yard.

"What?" He shook his head and reacted to the unexpected and aggressive behaviour by clenching his fists, and marching directly up to Bertie until their chests deliberately collided.

"Finn!" Bertie absorbed the challenging thud and refused to take a step backwards.

"Oh, that." Drake spat, using his body to press against Bertie.

"Him! It's him." Bertie leaned forward into Drake, determined he would not yield. "Not that."

"It was ages ago."

Their forehead slammed against each other's.

"Didn't you think I'd find out?" Bertie gritted his teeth.

"Think I care!" Drake goaded, pressing his head hard and trying to force Bertie to pull back.

"Why?" Bertie equalled Drake thrust. "Why did you do it?"

"He was just a dog." Suddenly Drake took half a step backwards. "Get over it and grow up." And pulled back his arm.

Bertie, being alert to the danger, swung his tight balled fist up from his waist and smashed it with all the force he could summon perfectly under Drake's chin before he had time to unleash his own ball of destruction. The impact rocked his head and he instantly staggering backwards with his swinging arm flailing through the icy air. Drake's senses were scrambled and his vision crippled with flashes of blinding brilliance.

133

He spat out a mouth full of blood through his split lips and before he had time to understand what had happened to him Bertie unleased a follow up blow to his face which rendered him useless and dropped him uncontrollably to the cold floor.

The loud crack of his back crashing to the cobbles echoed through the rear yards of South Cliff, but it did not deter Bertie from instantly following up with a swinging foot which violently and destructively hurled into Drake's exposed ribs.

He looked down at the rascal with hate and condemnation. His mind twisted by the sudden obsessive hatred of Drake spawned a hideous tirade of abuse which resulted in Bertie kicking Drake over and over until he was breathless and the blooded sagged heap moaning on the cobbles was drifting into oblivion.

"That's for Finn." He turned away unsatisfied. The air tasted foul in his mouth and his skinned knuckles smarted so much he involuntary rubbed them. He took a deep breath, the cold air searing his lungs, then he looked up as he walked out through the gate, hoping to see a shooting star or a celestial shimmering to confirm his vengeance had God's approval, but to his dismay he glimpsed Millie's pale face looking out of her bedroom window.

The moonlight shining full in her face, she flurried her brow and turned away with such speed that her long dark hair, which cascaded around her bare shoulders, wafted behind her like a wind-blown cloak. He did not know how long she'd been there or what she'd seen or heard. He cussed several times, but unashamedly he walked with his back straight and his head held high, all the time wondering if she would ever understand or forgive his brutality.

Chapter 18

The sky thundered, and the fields glowed red within Bertie's battle field nightmare. Screams wailed out from every bunker and bloodied dark trenches. The torture disturbed him so much he rolled over to try to dispel the dream with pleasant thoughts of swimming with Finn. However, his eyelids, disturbed by the orange glow which radiated through the flimsy curtains and danced around the ceiling and walls, continued to flicker. Suddenly his head bolted from the pillow, and he rubbed his face to awaken himself and shake away the fog of sleep and the fright of the nightmare. With his heart racing, at first he struggled to make sense of his surroundings, but muffled words from outside replaced the echoing death screams, and realising the nightmare was not over, he leaped out from the bed to pull open the curtains.

"No!" He yelled as his eyes locked onto the raging fire on the cliff top, and grabbing only his trousers, he ran from the bedroom and descended their stairs so fast his feet only landed on every fourth step. Bouncing off the hallway wall and leaning against the kitchen door, he pulled up his trousers and snapped into his braces he asked himself.

"What's happened?"

He barged through the small gathering of curious onlookers, who shuddered under their shawls, to race across the white ice blanket, the grass crunching beneath his bare feet.

"How can this be?" He glared at the furnace, it's sky stretching flames fully engulfing and ravaging the once cliff top Command Centre.

"No! No, no." He felt helpless. There was nothing he could do. The heat stung his face and the winter's blast froze his back as he watched the cracking wood and rising ambers of destruction sparkle against the blackness of the cliff top sky.

He dropped his head into his hands and pressed the heel of his palm against his eyes to hold back tears. He did not hear Millie's feet step through the crisp, long grass to stand beside him, but he felt her wrap her father's oversize jacket around his shivering shoulders.

"Blimey." She muttered, her eyes marvelling at the ferocious furnace and her pupils reflecting the raging blaze which danced mesmerizingly against the black canvas. "The stove was dead." She sounded uncertain. "And we didn't leave any candles burning."

"There was nothing." Smashing his fist into the ground, he raised his face to the blaze.

"I don't understand it." Like the shadowy figures at the edge of the village, she could not distract herself from the appeal of the fervent intensity of obliteration.

"I do." Said Bertie.

"What?" Her eyes remained fixed on the searing danger.

"Drake!" He shouted, turning his head to squint at the silhouettes in the distance.

"No. He wouldn't..........Would he?" She hoped he hadn't, but she suspected he could.

Bertie didn't reply. He did not want to say anything, and he did not want to hear Millie naively defend him.

136

He straightened himself and glared into her eyes. Anger had replaced his pain and, startled by the penetrating lour, Millie stepped aside to let him pass.

"The uniforms, our James's letters, the magazines and Newt's binoculars, all gone." The jacket fell from his shoulders and to the ground as he bumped passed her and set off to hunt down Drake. "The bastard has destroyed the lot."

He knew the coward would not be found amongst the crowd, who now beginning to lose interest were sauntering back to the warmth and the comfort of their beds, and he knew he would not appear at his bedroom window, no matter how loud he shouted or how many stones he threw at the glass.

Now totally despondent, he too returned home to bathe his gashed feet and warm up his numbed bones, knowing his Ma would still be unconscious and oblivious to the commotion, and even worse, Drake would be sniggering somewhere in the darkness.

Early the following morning Bertie was sifting through the still warm pile of ash and charcoal when he saw a bleary-eyed Newt trampling through the frozen hard grass.

"It's all over Newt."

"Over?" Newt replied, nearing the acrid stink of sulphur.

"There is no more TVC." Bertie kicked a pile of ash to reveal a glow of smouldering cinders.

"Don't say that." Newt drew level with him and together they bent over the warm ash to rub their hands above the rising warmth.

"It doesn't have to be this way." Newt seemed to plead.

"Time to do other things." Bertie's mind was set. No longer was he going to waste his time playing childish war games. Although Drake's slur had hurt, he knew he was right, and they had outgrown the adventure.

"It doesn't have to be the end." Newt prodded a long piece of charred wood and stirred it into the ash until a small flame ignited.

"There is nothing else." Bertie added a few fragments of scorched wood to stoke the fire.

"My Pa says we were all doing a sterling job."

Bertie looked at Newt and smiled, recognising it was the first time he'd heard anything about his Pa since he had read James's letters.

"We haven't done anything meaningful except give out some brandy and stock up wood."

"Well, then." Newt rubbed his hands over the fire. "Let's do something else."

"Like what?" Bertie eyed the girls running towards them in the distance.

"I dunno." Newt stared into the flames, hoping the mesmerising flickers would incite his imagination. "Let's rebuild it bigger and better. James showed us how."

"Nah. No point there is nothing interesting to see here." Bertie continued to rub and warm his hands above the rising heat. "It's obvious now. If the Germans are going to come, they'll land further up the coast." He paused, hearing Millie's and Lily's steps crunch at his rear. "They aren't interested in anything here."

"What you doing?" The girls cautiously asked together as their eyes absorbing the pile of charred wood and ashes of the now ruined Command Centre.

"Getting warm." Still embarrassed by his actions from last night, Bertie did not turn to greet Millie.

"What a mess." Lily said what the others all thought.

"We're going to do something else." Newt stood and turned, anticipating the girl's interest.

"Something else?" They giggled as again they unintentionally answered in unison.

"Something bigger." Newt stretched out his arms in front of his chest to demonstrate his vision.

"Bigger?" Lily wondered.

"Like what?" Bertie cynically shook his head. "Another den where there are no children to play? A church where there is no one left to pray? A pub where there is no one to come and drink? There's no one left here to build anything for." He shouted as he kicked out at the piles of charred wood to scatter ash high in all directions.

"Oh, Bertie stop. Stop it right now." Millie asserted as she walked to his side. "We all know you're upset, but..." She raised her right hand and rested it on his forearm to calm him.

"Upset! You're bloody right. I'm upset." He cut in. "I'm upset we've…. I've wasted all this time and effort for nothing."

"It's not been for nothing." Newt despondently muttered as he waved away the cloud of eye smarting ash which had followed Bertie's wild swinging foot.

However, it was Millie's authorative call, which caused all their heads to swivel in her direction. "Then let us not waste any more time doing something for nothing. Let's build something worthwhile."

"That's what I said." Newt frowned.

Millie's liveliness buoyed Lily and Newt's frame of mind and roused their enthusiasm. Eagerly and instinctively, they gathered around her.

"Such as?" Bertie said as he began to walk away and towards the winding path which led down into Horseshoe Cove.

"What about a viewing shelter where everyone can come in the summer and enjoy the view of the sea?" Lily beamed as the three of them followed Bertie to the cliff top.

"With a bandstand …… and we could organise a summer fete." Newt grinned.

Seeing the dark entrance to Quintal's Cave at the foot of the cove, Bertie stopped and held his breath 'Finn.'

Nearing the cave evoked his last harrowing image of his trusted companion, and instantly his eyes welled and his heart pounded. He remained motionless for a few moments, not knowing if he could continue, but hearing the gang just a few steps behind him, he flexed his muscles taut and grimaced to defy the anguish to slowly, continue on down the slippery steep and winding narrow path.

Millie, being the only one in the gang who knew what had happened to Finn, saw Bertie's hesitation, and trying to distract him from the ghastly memory. "A library?" She blurted. "We could ask for donations of old or unwanted books."

"A games hall?" Newt suggested enthusiastically. "Maybe we could borrow a dart board and build our own billiards table."

"A Hall?" Lily screwed up her face.

"A dance hall?" Millie sought to sustain the newfound optimism. "If we could get our hands on an old piano, I could play a few tunes."

Disregarding the excited proposals, Bertie's eyes avoided Quintal's dark chasm to concentrate on the fresh wintery deliverance of planks of wood, smashed up crates, fish baskets, rope and smashed bottles. He walked cautiously amongst the seaweed and away from his reinvigorated friends as they called out one enthusiastic idea after another. Not once did he raise his eyes from the surface as he tried desperately to ignore the urge to glance up and beyond the entrance of the cave.

A wild thought spasmed his imagination. 'Maybe if Finn can make it back to camp, he can run away and find his way home.'

He cursed his stupid daydream and kicked out to flip over with his foot a crate stamped with a huge red 'fragile' warning. A soggy piece of floating newspaper caught his eye, and he stretched out his leg and twisted until he could prevent the print from floating away with his foot and drag it along the icy water without lifting it from the rock pool. Arching his back and being careful not to get wet, he used his forefinger to unfold the crumpled sheet, but he cursed his luck as unravelling the sheet, he saw the back page rather than a war headline, as he had hoped.

He cast away the page and began to rise, but as doing so he glimpsed a picture advertising 'Hadley Holmes's Travelling Vaudeville'. He lowered himself again to stare at length at the picture of a scantily clad dancer and a chained muscle man.

"Music hall." He mouthed.

"Bertie?" Millie looked at him.

"A music hall." Straightening his back, he repeated louder.

"A music hall?" Millie's eye's widened.

"Yes, a music hall." They neared each other. "Where together we can put on a type of vaudeville act for the locals."

"That's what I said. A hall." Newt reiterated.

"No. A music hall where we can put on a show." Bertie carefully lifted the paper out of the cold water.

"But we can't sing." Lily heard the suggestion.

"No, but I can play a few tunes and we can learn to sing." Millie humoured Bertie.

"Sing!" Newt skipped over a rock pool to join the chat. "I'm not singing."

"Me too!" Lily shuddered and shook her head.

"There's lots of other things we can do." Millie enthused.

"What like?" Newt shrugged his shoulders.

 "Maybe we could act out some scenes from famous plays." She proposed whilst giggling out the words of Beatrice Adel. "Oh cometh darling. Cometh with me unto paradise."

"Or we can some do readings." Lily joined in the fun and recited from Oscar Wilde's Dorian Grey. "When we are happy, we are always good, but when we are good, we are not always happy."

"We can do both." Bertie laughed, and Millie and Lily ran to his side.

"My reading's not too good." Newt worried about his stutter.

"Then tell a few jokes." Bertie encouraged." Learn some magic tricks."

"We can do lots of things. Learn to play an instrument from a book or practice juggling." Millie put both her hands on Newt's shoulders and gave him a shake. "What about a puppet show?"

"Puppet show?" He seemed petrified.

"Punch and Judy." Lily roared eagerly. "He's behind you!"

"Oh, dear." Newt shook his head.

"We could turn it into the English bashing the Huns." Bertie tapped his clenched fists together and laughed. "That's the way you do it."

"Come on, Newt." Lily urged.

"It's only a bit of fun." Her hand still on his shoulders, Millie tried to reassure him, and she gave him a gentle squeeze.

"Look, Newt, there's nowhere for them to go anymore." Nearing him, Bertie deliberately tried to stir his inner sense of duty. "Nowhere for our folks to have a drink, and a bit of fun and chatter like they did in the old days when they all went to the Ship. They need something like this to lift their spirits." He consciously avoided mentioning the invalid, who was once his cheerful father. "It will take a lot of time and hard work, but we can do this."

"And it'll need us all to get involved." Lily said.

"What about Drake?" Newt asked.

"I'm sure he'll come round." Bertie looked at Millie's impassive face. "Eventually."

"It's you we need, Newt." Millie declared without responding to the mischievous glint in Bertie's eye. "You're a natural entertainer."

"I guess we could still put up a dartboard and maybe put the billiards table in the back." Hearing he was needed by his friends pleased him, and finally the worried scowl lifted and he too began to smile.

"Yes, and look" Bertie swung his arm to point at the rocks where he'd seen an unbroken bottle of stout. "We can collect up plenty more of these and give them free drinks."

"Come on Newt. Help us do it." Millie's eyes widened and tilting her head, she turned over her bottom lip to impersonate sadness. "Do it for those with now where to go."

"A tribute for those who are not with us." Bertie added.

"We'd have to give it a name." Lily announced.

Newt titled his head and raised his eyebrows at Bertie. "Name it after James. One of our own brave South Cliff lads."

"What about naming it after poor Hubert Alderthay?" Bertie proposed.

"Hubert's Hall." Lily giggled.

"The Alderthay." Millie revised.

"Seems more fitting for the poor fella." Bertie seconded.

After a moment's pause, Newt smiled. "Yes. Count me in. Let's build The Alderthay." Nodding, he was immediately engulfed in a collective embrace and cheers echoed around the cove.

Bertie was the first who broke the group hug to explore last night's haul and pointing across the cove, he hollered. "There's plenty of wood, so we can get started right away."

"We'll be able to get almost everything we need right here." Millie responded as she too scanned the wet shore.

"I'll write down of all our ideas." Lily announced.

"And I'll practice my piano skills." Millie confirmed, following Bertie's steps carefully from one boulder to the next.

"Once we decide what we are going to do, I can also list what we are going to need." Lily continued now tracking Millie's imprints in the sand.

"What are these doing in here?"

Hearing Newt's loud call in the distance, all three of them stopped and turned their heads to see Newt standing in the entrance to Quintals Cave holding aloft Finns bowl, his toy and a large marrow bone.

Chapter 19

24th September

Dear Ma & Bertie

In the trenches we eat, sleep and live with the dead. The air stinks and the streams are red with blood and the land is grey with rotting flesh. It is now so bad we cannot tell the flesh from filth. During the day we are pinned down by constant rat tat tat and when the darkness falls we crawl out into the mud to cause as much mayhem for the Huns as we possibly can.

Our food is infested and often we wake up with the rats nibbling our flesh, as if we too were dead.

Thank God the latest rumours are we are being sent from the hell hole to help the French at Ypres.

James.

Bertie shuddered. The letters home were now infrequent, gruesome and very brief, but Bertie and his Ma were at least thankful knowing James was still alive.

Strange as it may seem, and he dare not speak about it to anyone Bertie was still more worried about Finn than James, and whenever he could not fight away the yearning for his furry friend, and the longing to once again stroke and kiss his snout tears still spilled down his cheeks.

The long dire winter didn't help his sorrow, and boredom began to despair him, so out of desperation, and to save his mind and soul he did not wait until the weekends, like Millie and Lily to scavenge amongst the washed up treasure, and often he would use the intermittent moon glow to start shovelling and hauling away the charred ruins and ashes of the Command Centre. Occasionally alongside him, eager to help, Newt would sneak out of his bedroom window to assist him, and working like a trooper, he too worked until late into the night, filling the barrow with ash and collecting fresh delivers of timber from the sea.

Finally, as the spring strew it's warmth across the cliff tops and the sun began to cast its radiance earlier every morning so too did Bertie and Newt expand their toil, and by the time the new shoots of growth greened the fields had prettied the hedgerows the ruins of the old Command Centre had been removed and a new larger base of beach rocks the width of South Cliff's main street had been laid.

With the extended daylight and the increasing pile of wood on the cliff top, now intrigued the locals began to gaze on from a distance with mystified silence and lots of chin rubbing and head scratching as they failed to comprehend the purpose of the new activity.

A couple of days later Millie informed the gang their parents had held a secret meeting to discuss the appearance of the sizable frame work which had begun to develop on the horizon between the green cliff top and the blue of the sky, and then with boundless delight she revealed they had agreed not to interfere so long as the girls and Newt did their home studies and their fieldwork as and when it was required.

She chuckled with pride, repeating most of them believed their hobby would keep them out of mischief and help them learn useful skills.

Old Man Corney appeared from time to time again to pry and skit, often giggling at his own poor jokes regarding the building of Noah's Ark, but he soon merrily left the labourers to continue with their graft once his fingers were clutching tight around a fine bottle from the latest waves.

All the time for play had ceased, but no one grumbled or wanted to rest. They were all too busy enjoying the vertical emergence of their new project. Every four feet, they rooted deep posts to stabilise the frame, and they nailed and mortised planks to rugged studs. Banging echoed around the coves, and the sound of cutting and sawing was carried over the village by the recurrent spring breeze.

As Bertie worked diligently on the wood workings, a quiet, yet persistent voice guided his every step. It was the voice of James detailing every precise instruction with encouraging resolve and creativity. No longer was the task just about constructing a building of significance. To Bertie it was now about preserving the essence of the poor lost souls who had forfeited their lives for the safety of their loves ones.

Millie brought sandwiches and drinks, Lilly played her mouth organ and in the frustrating periods where they had to wait for the tide to wash in the next supply of wood, they discussed ideas, shared jokes and practised routines. Still, no one openly mentioned the absence of Drake until one day Newt told the gang he'd heard a rumour that Drake had run away to sign up and fight the Germans.

Although eyes flickered between the girls, still no one mentioned their friend's sudden and strange disappearance, but Bertie knew. He was sure Millie had quietly recalled what she had seen on that brutal night to her pals.

The undertaking of collecting wood, measuring, cutting, shaping and joining it had now become a labour of love, devotion and unwavering determination, proving testimony to the gang's unity and friendship which together bound their will to succeed.

At the end of each exhausting day they relived their chafed areas, cooled the sunburn, and swilled off the sawdust by frolicking and bathing in the sea. Their hard routine continued daily with merry chatter and harmony, and by the beginning of summer Bertie was securing the struts and attaching the outer sheathing.

"Looks great." Newt complemented.

"Amazing." Grinned Lilly.

"Great job Bertie." Millie added in-between a blast of 'Let me call you sweetheart' which she quietly asked Lily to play on her mouth organ.

Colour surged into Bertie's face, but hiding his embarrassment and trying to ignore the tease, he unnecessarily continued slamming his hammer against a sunken nail.

"Bloody hell!" Newt stuttered as he ducked.

"What's that?" Lily gasped after hearing something thud into the long grass ten strides to her left.

"Is it a bird?" Millie thought she caught a glimpse of a falling object.

A Boy, a Dog and the Great War

Clutching the hammer as a weapon, Bertie moved alongside the others and slowly led them towards the disturbance in the long grass.

"It is. It is a bird." Millie huffed with both relief and pity.

"Is it dead?" Lily dropped her mouth organ into her blouse pocket.

"Hurt maybe." Bertie leaned for a better inspection and his body shadowed the grey bird.

"What is it?" Newt also tentatively arched lower.

"It's a bird. I've just told you." Millie carefully lowered to her knees next to it.

"I know it's a bird." Newt frowned. "But what sort and why has it landed here?"

"It's a pigeon and the poor little fella is exhausted." Bertie said, nearing his face to within a few inches of it's ruffled up feathers. "And I think it's in shock."

"How can you tell?" Both Newt and Lily jointly asked.

"Well, it's still breathing. Long slow breaths in, quick pants out." Bertie confirmed as he scrutinized it's wheezing.

Millie smiled. She did not doubt his wisdom.

"Have we got anything to wrap it in?" Bertie looked at the girls, hoping they would scour the building site, but Millie instantly offered.

"Here, use this." She untied her neck scarf.

"Millie!" Lily eye's widened with disgust.

"It will wash."

"Are you sure?" Bertie asked.

"Take it." Millie held out the scarf. "And be careful it doesn't bite."

"Bite," Bertie smiled, taking the scarf. "It might peck a little, but it won't bite." He slid the scarf under the lame bird. It was too weak to struggle, and he easily lifted it from the grass to inspect it's beak, wings and body carefully with his finger.

"It's starving."

"Starving?" Newt repeated.

"Yes, it's breast bone's prominent." Then he shouted. "Oh, wow."

"What?" Newt, Lily and Millie all said at once.

"What's wrong?"

"What is it?"

"What have you found?"

"Only a bloody canister." He enthused, tapping the small silver container which was attached to the pigeon's leg. "It's carrying a message."

"Message?"

"Are you sure?"

"Yes. It's a homing pigeon. I've seen lots of them in the magazine." He did not break his stare from the canister. "The army is using them to send messages."

"Why kind of message?" Newt gaped.

"I don't bloody know, but it could be important." Bertie carefully folded the scarf around the bird to keep it warm.

"What do we do now?"

"What are you going to do with it, Bertie?"

"Shall we eat it?" Newt's tongue rolled across his bottom lip and he smacked his mouth open and shut.

"Arr!"

"Disgusting!" The girls screamed at him.

"Well. When did you last eat any meat?" Unintentionally, Newt rubbed his rumbling stomach.

"No, we are not going to eat him."

Together, the girls sighed as Bertie spoke.

"We're going to try and get the little fella to eat and drink something." He pulled the bird close to his chest to cradle it. "Then we'll take him to the station in Trewin tomorrow."

"Can I come?" Newt shouted.

"Me too?" Requested Millie.

"All of us." Lily added.

"If you like, but won't be very exciting. There not going to tell us anything."

"Not even if it's important or not?" Newt stammered for the first time that day.

"Doubt it." Ignoring Newt's excited stammer, Bertie continued. "I think they'll just take the little cylinder to the garrison in Falmouth."

"And what about the pigeon?" Millie worried, and Bertie simply shrugged his shoulders and raised his eyebrows.

"Oh, I do hope the little fella's a hero." Lily's mind had flooded with thoughts of adventure.

"All the way from France?" Newt frowned as he elbowed her gently in the ribs for being foolish.

"We've got some dripping and left over crushed carrots in the larder." Said Millie.

"Let's go." Bertie did not hesitate.

Chapter 20

The dark blue uniformed officer at the police station in Trewin did not introduce himself. Looking almost bewildered, he just listened to why four youngsters appeared to be wasting his time, and grumpily accepting the crude carry box which Bertie had assembled to carry the pigeon, he quickly ushered them back out of the station door thanking them for their diligence.

Miserably, they cussed the officer for his inconsiderate behaviour, and trudged back to South Cliff to dispel their disappointment by occupying themselves once more with hard graft. The girls measured the wood, Bertie cut it and Newt assembled the pieces, and held them in position for Bertie to nail secure. Every hour or so Newt and the girls would swap duties, but so intense was their determination to get the walls finished, they worked tirelessly with few pauses or refreshment breaks.

A faint buzzing noise distracted Millie, and urging them all to stop the lively chatter, and asking Bertie to hold still his hammer for a moment, she angled her head to improve her hearing.

"I hear it too." Lily affirmed.

"Big bloody bee, but I can't see it." Bertie flicked glances around the flower tops of the surrounding grass.

"Nor I." Newt did the same as the buzzing sound gradually increased.

"Wait, a moment." Millie lifted her face up to the sky. "Is it coming from over there?" She pointed high into the distance above the sea.

Bertie rubbed the inside of his ears with his finger to stop the din from the hammer and walked towards his skyward looking friends.

"What on earth?"

Squinting from the bright sun and shielding their eyes with their hands together, they searched the sky to identify the strange whining noise.

"What can it be?" Newt shouted as the whirling sound grew louder from above.

Suddenly they all threw themselves forward and dived face first into the long grass as, appearing with great speed out from the blaze of the clear sun, was a plane.

Having never seen one before, the girls screamed with fear and covered their ears with their hands and closed their eyes.

"Oh, no!" Millie muttered into the soil.

"What is it?" Too afraid to look up, Newt stuttered.

"Germans." Millie, fearing invasion, replied with a tremor in her voice.

The noise grew louder and seeing the shadow of the plane pass over them, Bertie craned his neck and shot a glance skywards.

"It's ok." He shouted after seeing the pilot waving at them. "It's a plane, and it's one of ours."

"A plane. How do you know?" Nervously, Newt curved his back so he could glance up without rising out from the tall grass.

"Seen them." Bertie was the first to rise.

"Where?" Newt hesitated to move.

"In the papers and magazine." Bertie waved back at the pilot as the plane began to rise into a vast expanse of white fluff which drifted to cover the summer blue and cast it's fast moving shadows along the cliff top fields.

"Are you sure?" Newt remained prone.

"Well, it's not another bloody pigeon is it?" Bertie laughed now turning back and seeing the heads of his friends peeking out above the tall, rippling grass.

"Didn't know they flew that high." Millie patted her dress as she fully emerged into view.

"And how do you know it's one of ours?" Still sceptical, Newt continued. "And what's it doing flying over here?"

"Is he lost?" Belatedly, Lilly began to wave back as she speculated.

"It's an Armstrong Whitworth." Shouted the policeman above the distant humming of the low-flying biplane.

In the excitement, they did not see the policeman cycling towards them.

"Old type ......FK2." He added, lifting his leg over the frame of the bike to dismount. "No need to be afraid. He's probably just doing a routine fly over."

Confused, the gang looked at each other as they straightened and brushed the grass off their clothing.

157

"I've come to tell you about Eric." With care, he rested down his cycle and began to walk towards them.

Staring blankly and flicking their gazes between themselves and the policeman, the gang mouthed together.

"Eric?"

"Yes Eric. Our little champion." Recognising from their bewildered expressions they had no idea who he was talking about, he shook his head and added. "The injured pigeon you brought in last week..... Eric the homing pigeon. I've come to bring you some good news about him."

"Eric?" They giggled as they too walked to greet the policeman.

"Yes, it turns out our little Eric is a war hero, and you are all to be congratulated for your actions." His cheeks creased with a huge smile.

Although she understood what he said, Lily could not help repeat his words. "Hero .... congratulated .... actions."

"Yes, delivering the little chap to the station is the best thing you could have done for your country, and you are to be commended for it."

"What?" "Huh?" "How?" "Why?" They gasped at once.

Barraged by the questions, he removed his helmet and wiped his brow with his sleeve, and then he held his breath. "I shouldn't be telling you this, but if you swear to secrecy. "He raised his eyebrows and tapped the end of his nose. "It turns out the little homer you saved."

"Eric?" The amusing name leaped from Newt's mouth before he thought to stop it.

"Yes Eric. He was dispatched to deliver a message from the crew of the Boadicea. I'll not tell you their position, but they had been breached in an attack by a German U boat and were sinking slowly." His tone was low and solemn. "Stranded and without power they would all have died if it wasn't for your good sense of duty and Eric's immense bravery." He nodded and his sternness relaxed into a smile to show his appreciation for their efforts. "You can all be very proud of yourselves, and by the way of a special thank you, the Mayor has invited you and all of your families to have lunch with him at Burlington's next Thursday."

Beaming smiles immediately stretched the mouths of the gang as the invite to the restaurant in Trewin thrilled them.

"1pm prompt." He cast in their direction another smile, saluted and returned to his bike. Then, raising one leg over the cycle frame, and balancing himself on the peddle he looked at the stationary youngsters once more and said. "Oh, and you'll probably be seeing more of them flying over now."

"Pigeons?" Newt stupidly asked.

"No." The officer shook his head as he fixed his helmet. "Planes! They're starting to make them in the old factory over in Pendale." Then, propelling himself away with a leg thrust, he shouted. "See you all at Burlington's and don't be late."

With a wave, he left the gang to reflect in amazement at their achievement and marvel at Eric's courage.

159

"I'm going to celebrate." Millie excitedly broke the silence.

"Me too. I'm going to make a new ribbon for my hair." Lily giddily declared.

"No silly. Not like that. I'm going to properly celebrate." Millie's eye contained a mischievous look none of them had ever seen before.

"Celebrate? What do you mean?" Newt gave her half a smile.

"Those cigarettes we've been saving." She raised her eyebrows. "I'm going to have one."

"No…. Really?" Newt's jaw hung loose. "Are you really going to smoke?"

"Why not?" Bertie joined in. "Let's all have one." He energetically linked Millie's arm and spun her on her heels to face the cliff top and whilst in the same euphoric moment he raced her to Quintal's Cave, leaving Newt and Lily struggling to keep up with them.

"Oh, I feel dizzy." Lily said, blowing out a mouthful of smoke.

"I feel sick." Newt's face had paled.

"Me too." Millie's forehead crinkled and closing her eyes, a shudder cause goose bumps on her skin.

"You've all dragged it in too fast." Said Bertie, himself feeling a little giddy. "You need to slow down and hold the smoke in your mouth and at the back of your throat before swallowing it."

He gave a demonstration.

"Oh, I can't do that." Lily gagged and her cigarette shook in her fingers.

"Then try taking a small breath and blow it out without you swallowing it." Again Bertie displayed his expertise.

Millie followed his instruction, but screwing up her face, she threw her cigarette into rocks and jumped to her feet.

"Arr!" She screamed and skipping across the large boulders in the base of the cave, she heaved out the contents of her stomach into a small rock pool near to the entrance.

"Well, that didn't work." Newt giggled, watching her arch over and spit several times, all very unladylike.

"You're not used to it, that's all." Bertie once more sucked on the cigarette until the tip glowed on his face.

"And you are?" Millie wiped her mouth with salty water from a pool, then she straightened and turned to watch him enjoy the thrill.

"I've had one or two before." He inhaled again. "With our James." Smoke blasted out from his nostrils. "You'll soon get used to it."

"No, I won't. It tastes vile and the smell is disgusting." She screwed up her face. They're horrid little things, and I shall never touch one again."

"We'll see." Bertie wasn't looking at her. He had become distracted by the newspaper fragment he had saved and pulled from his pocket.

His imagination dominated his attention as he gazed extensively through the smoke and at the picture of the scantily clad dancer and the chained muscle man from Hadley Holmes's Travelling Vaudeville act. He read out the list of the entertainers until his eyes settled on the vocalist 'Laney Dove'.

Chapter 21

The celebratory meal was greatly received by families of the gang, however there were two absentees from the list of invitees and two replacement leeches. Both Bertie's Ma and Newt's Pa did not wish to attend and so Old Man Corney and his wife, in return for providing the transportation cart to Trewin, had quickly presented themselves as replacements.

Before the meal was served, the Mayor commended the gang for their astuteness with a lengthy speech, and an officer from the navy presented all four of them with a certificate for their achievement.

Although proud to receive her certificate, Millie told the officer she felt undeserving of the reward and that it was Eric who should be honoured. With a great smile the officer agreed, and an associate from the back room walked to the dining area to place Eric's cage at the head of the table so he could sit formally between the Mayor and the navy officer. The officer then held aloft a medal and said to Millie.

"Maybe you would like to present Eric with this."

"Oh my."

Colour surged into her face, and at first she radiated with astonished joy, but then after a moment's reflection with grace and a polite humbleness she mustered a few words of gratitude on behalf of the chirpy hero, and then with fumbling embarrassment she fastened the blue ribboned medal to Eric's cage.

Unfortunately, the glorious meal left a bitter taste in the mouths of the four honourees from South Cliff as departing Burlington's they over heard the Officer inform the mayor that Eric was not going to be afforded an early retirement because pigeons with his abilities were still desperately need on the front line.

By the end of the month Bertie had assembled and started fitting the ceiling joist, outriggers and rafters. He'd had a long, frustrating delay waiting for more wood, but the hellish weekend tide had left behind enough material for him to complete the frame of the roof.

All thoughts about watching out for German ships were now forgotten and his entire efforts and focus were to complete the build before the onset of the winter. In addition to his despondency at missing and worrying about Finn, he now found he had to ignore gawkers who came from miles around to ridicule and scoff at what they could not understand. Daily, he toiled and, remaining steadfast, he shunned the scepticism and mockery which was yelled in his direction.

It was always dark by the time he returned home to read the latest letter from James and, as usual, his Ma was dozing in the fireside chair with the familiar black bottle in her hand and an open letter on her lap.

13th June

Dear Ma & Bertie

I start my letter by asking you to forgive me for I have now learned not to mourn my fellow comrades, for I have said goodbye to so many lately, all because of this war.

Only last night a chap I was jolly with took a direct hit to the head, which was a great mercy for him, for he did not suffer as he might, and as so many poor devils have done so.

Out here we have all become soulmates of death as we eat, sleep and live with dying, the dead and the rotting corpses. The air stinks of decay and the land is grey and brown. No longer can we tell flesh from filth. The roads hereabout are full, night and day, with new ammunition trucks, and reinforcements of infantrymen all slogging up here to stand beside us in the trenches, poor beggars. There is never any peace or quiet, for there is a constant barrage of artillery and machine gun fire, so we are all so desperately tired and in need of a warm mattress and a restful night.

Tonight though, I am thoroughly encouraged because, thank God, I hear the Hun is on the retreat at last, and we expect his guns will slowly grow quieter.

Thank you for the letters and parcels. They give me great comfort when I am crawling on my belly through the blood and mud.

Love James.

Bertie silently put the letter back in her lap and shaking his head, he thought of Finn struggling in the mire as around him machine-gun bullets pounded indiscriminately into the mud and the dying. He cussed his Ma, the Germans, the army, the war and God, and then, knowing sleep would evade him, he went back out to sit on the cliff tops, and stare out into the blackness.

Chapter 22

Rain, stormy gales and flashes of distant lightening over the black sea accompanied the promise of a thunder on opening night, adding to the further doubts to the gang's anxiety.

"Do you think anyone will actually come?" Asked Millie, holding tight her brolly over herself and Lily as they dashed towards the door.

"Hope so."

"Bloody weather." Bertie was inside already waiting for them with the door handle in his grasp. "It's bad enough to keep the animals inside." He added, pulling back the door for the girls and scowling out into the dark.

"We told them we were raising money for the injured Soldiers and Sailors Christmas gift fund." Millie said, shaking the water from her shoulders and the brolly.

"Made it perfectly clear on the flyers." Lily added.

"We even promised free refreshments." Newt appeared from the back room.

The moaning and whistling gusts spliced through the panel boards, causing timbers to squeak and groan, and the sagging door hanging on it's already rusty grating hinges eased back and then slammed hard back into it's frame. The wall candles flickered a jaundiced quivering light across the dozen rickety pews that were waiting for parents and neighbours who had all received Millie's and Lily's handmade invitations to attend Saturday night's free theatrical entertainment.

166

Together they all nervously waited and paced the creaking stage, hoping for someone to venture through the lantern's enticing entrance. Fingers crossed, with glances to heaven they appealed to God for someone to turn up, however together they sighed and doubted.

They had all worked tirelessly hard building the small theatre and practicing their routines. For months, in the periods when they had to wait for wood, and they had gotten bored with practising their routines, they had collected and saved crates of alcohol to give out free welcoming drinks, all provided by the sea wreaks and a lot of manual effort. Now bottles of beer and spirits, which had survived the crashing against the rocks were lined up the long shelf at the rear end of the building along with a neat row of tin cups which hadn't made it over the water to France, and in the small space beneath the shelves, laid out with six hand crafted stools waited a tray of old dominos and a stack of cards, both Newt's smart ideas.

On the edge of the tiny stage Lily and Millie sat with their legs dangling and frustratedly swinging back and forth. Newt fidgeted with the curtain and pole they had erected at the back of the stage to give them some privacy, and Bertie, he couldn't wait any longer.

He impatiently jumped down from the crated stage and went outside to stare across the dark fields toward South Cliff, all the time looking for signs of activity. Besides, there wasn't anything else he could do now.

The girls had perfectly laid out all the hand crafted furnishings, and Newt was applying the final touches to the changing area and he wasn't required for the show until the final act.

All the rehearsals had been meticulously finalized, and the girls were ready and waiting to open the show by singing 'It's Tulip Time in Holland', 'Keep the Home Fires Burning', and 'It's a Long Way to Tipperary, then Newt was to take over the stage by telling some jokes whilst he was juggling, and bringing an end to the first half of the show, Lily had memorised to recite Act one, Scene one from Shakespeare's 'A Midsummer Night's Dream'. Should the event be successful, as they all hoped, and another production arranged, she agreed to continue with the other three acts.

After a short interlude, the four of them would perform their adaptation of 'England Expects' by Edward Kenblauch. The story had amused Millie when she read the book given to her by an aunt who lived in London, and now she wanted to share the story with her friends and neighbours.

Impatiently Bertie paced around the outside of the building, the sea wind's raw edge blowing through his jumper and chilling his skin.

"Bloody weather." He grumbled. "Atrocious." He bent over to replace the donations buckets which had blown over and rolled away from the entrance. 'Nobody will come in this. Thank you, God.'

He looked up and squinted as now the rain blurred his eyes. The placard 'The Alderthay', freshly painted in red and white, and not yet full dry, swung back and forth on it's chains and banged loudly on the wooden panelled outer wall.

"Evening Bertie." Faced cloaked by his jacket, the unidentified man shocked Bertie as he hurried passed him to disappear inside the doorway.

"Great job Bertie."

"What you doing out here? You'll catch your death."

"Hope it all goes well."

He didn't see the small umbrella huddling group appear out of the darkness to scurry by and rush through the lantern lit doorway. Taken by surprise, his courteous reply caught in his throat, and he managed only a subtle nod, which no one saw.

'Well, bugger me………. Six people.' He shook the rain from his hair and inquisitively squinted again out into the blackness and towards another couple of black figures who had appeared in the distance. He smiled and ran back in to share the news with Millie, but she was busy helping the visitors out of their coats and to their seats, so he looked for Newt and Lily. He desperately wanted to share the elation with them, but they too were busy pouring out drinks. He ran back outside, and looked beyond the brollies of two more approaching figures, and he saw another group of people approaching. He closed his eyes and held his face up to the rain and smiled 'Thank you,' then he heard the thudding of hooves and the rattling of cart wheels behind him.

Turning his neck and shielding his eyes from the gust of rain with the flat of his hand in the distance he could just make out Old Man Corney face under the cover of a tarp and to his rear and crammed in shoulder to shoulder was a cart full of sodden town's folk. He ran across the mud to guide Corney's horse as near to the entrance as possible.

"Hope this is going to be worth it Bertie boy." Corney said then covering his mouth with his hand so only Bertie could hear his words he added. "The old hag's made me drive out to Trewin on a night like this."

169

Bertie still despised Corney, and he suspected he had only adhered to his wife's request for his own selfish gain.

"I'm sure you'll find something to warm you inside." He narrowed his eyes and nodded as he rushed to the rear of the cart to help the new arrivals step down.

Courteous nods and 'thanks you's met Bertie's cold and wet assisting hand, but once more suddenly his throat dried, and he could not find any words in response to the greetings as concealed within a shawl he glimpsed the face of Mrs Alderthay. She forced a smile, and thanked Bertie for his assistance, and then before proceeding any further, she arched back her head and looked up at the theatre sign above her as it swung in the wind. Bertie turned his face to the distant rumble and the flash which briefly illuminated and reflected from the sea. He began to count, but Mille distracted him.

"Bertie, all the benches are filling up." She shouted from the doorway with a huge, but anxious smile. "What are we to do?"

"Take the games table out and ask them all to huddle up tight." He nodded his head in the direction of the passing widow and opened his eyes wide to gesture that he wanted Millie to find a seat for the widow.

"Fill around the sides and the back wall." He turned back to look at the thunder, knowing she had understood.

"Or you can just send them right on back home."

Bertie didn't see the two dark uniformed men approach. He'd been too busy.

"Where they should be on a night like this."

"What?" Bertie swivelled away from the coastline. He did not recognise the two policemen.

"Don't you mean excuse me Sir?" Lambasted the nearest officer through his thick water dripping whiskers.

"Y ... yes. Excuse me." Flustered, he nervously wondered what to do or say. A lump seemed to block his throat, and he felt sick.

"Raising money for the war effort, are you son?" Said the other officer.

"Yes .... Err yes Sir."

"Illegally?"

"No." Bertie worried. "It's for the."

"We know who you're claiming it's for." Cut in the whisked man.

Suddenly he realised the officer's motivation and feeling helpless he feared all the gangs hard work would be in vain. Worst of all, he feared humiliation of letting everyone down, especially the young widow.

"I think we'd better take a look inside."

Bertie saw the man's moustache rise in the half light as he grinned.

"What? Why?" Bertie took a sidewards step to obstruct their view.

"Issuing alcohol without a license and collecting money all sound a little underhand to me."

The smirking officer dropped one hand onto Bertie's shoulder to bully him out of the way. "Now step aside and don't do anything foolish."

"We are just putting on a little show to raise some money for our boys in France." Lifting his chin challengingly, Bertie stood firm.

"Are you now?" The man's tone and rising eyebrows insinuated he had uncovered a sinister plot.

"It's just a bit of fun." Bertie inhaled.

"Fun is it? Concealing his majesty's goods." Menaced the other officer as he too moved up close to Bertie's face.

"Don't you think the army could put all this wood to good use?"

The officer with the detaining hand pulled back his face to allow his eyes to roll across the wooden creation.

"And other resources you have collected, or should I say, stolen to better use." The second officer coughed and raised one eyebrow.

"Well boy, stand aside." Shouted the lead man. "It's time to get on with it."

Bertie, holding both his gaze and his breath, remained firm and so the infuriated officer leaned threateningly close to his face.

"Oh, I see. Standing in the way of justice are we now, boy?"

'Oh no.' Bertie groaned within. The dejected pale faces of Millie, Lily, Newt and Mrs Alderthay replaced the raging features of the officer and he stepped aside.

Pulling back the door and placing one foot just inside the wet and muddy entrance, the officer immediately retracted his head and shouted to his colleague.

"I think we can safely halt proceedings here and confiscate the goods." He grinned at his colleague who, also displaying a tooth bearing smile, added.

"Put the resources to better use and save you, young man, the trouble of pleading your innocence to a magistrate."

"Nothing illegal going on here."

Bertie thought he recognised the deep tone which bellowed from the darkness.

"Sergeant?" Immediately withdrawing his advance into the entrance, the officer stopped and turned to scowl beyond Bertie.

"Just some friendly kids putting in a lot of hard work." Added the Sergeant as he approached into yellow spray of the lantern.

Bertie exhaled relief as he watched the oil light dance on the policeman who he had handed Eric into at the station in Trewin.

"But?" Stuttered the other officer.

"You heard me, constable." The Sergeant affirmed, dismounting from his bike.

"Don't you think we should check?" Shrugged the whiskered man as he baulked.

"We've been told they're serving alcohol." Swaggered his partner.

"I'm not in the habit of repeating myself." The Sergeant rested his bike against the corner of the theatre and, filling his lungs, he commandingly strode to the front of the constable. "This type of work is not under the remit of volunteers, so I suggest you two return to whence you came and leave matters here to the professionals."

"Don't you think we should at least."

The Sergeant shouted and lunged forward. "What I think is that I've already said enough." And without warning, the Sergeant grabbed the collar of the volunteer in the doorway, and dragged him away from the hue of the oil lantern.

"Now get back to Trewin." He ordered as he hurled the startled man directly into a collision with his stunned colleague. "And be quick about it!"

"No need to worry yourself, Bertie." The Sergeant smiled as, wiping his hands, he returned to the light. "We've got the commander of the Admiralty behind us." Then, looking towards the door, he added. "Room in there for one more?"

"Millie will find you a seat." Returning the smile Bertie opened the door, but he didn't follow or watch the Sergeant into the theatre. His attention had been caught by another congregation that had appeared on the horizon. Arched and huddling under shawls, scarfs and brollies, another group of people at the edge of the village were slowly trudging in his direction.

He squinted to count the numbers of silhouettes, and then he saw in the middle of the pack, and being assisted by two people, a man was hobbling on crutches.

174

He spun to warn Millie of the late arrivals, but as he did so his route to the doorway was blocked.

"I'm ashamed of what I did, Bertie." Drake confessed. "I'm sorry." He lowered his head to the dark. "Truly I am."

Bertie drew in a composing breath and balled his fists. He'd often thought about what he'd do when he saw Drake again and for a long moment he held the silence, and just stared at the shadowy traitor.

"We could do with a little help inside." He never thought the unforgiving reunion would be tonight.

"Doing what?" The flickering yellow from the lantern danced on his shamed face.

"Getting everyone seated and pouring drinks." He nodded towards the group, who were slowly lumbering towards them. "Millie will show you what to do."

"Thank you." Drake tilted his face to the darkness once again to hide his embarrassment.

"And tell Newt his Pa's is on his way." He shouted as Drake eagerly leaped inside.

He stared at the nearing huddle and wondered if his own Ma was cloaked within the pack, and then once more he looked across the black to see at the flickers of brilliance which flashed from intermittently within the black clouds, and reflected off the shiny water. 'Better hurry.' But it wasn't just the stormy weather, and the opening nights nerves which bothered him.

Earlier that day, the post boy delivered a letter, and although it resembled the regular army envelopes, the letters on the delivery address did not match James's writing.

Afraid to open the letter Bertie's Ma thrust it into his hands, and told him to read it, however already being late for opening night, and not wanting a further delay he slid the envelope inside his pocket, and telling her it was nothing to worry about he sprinted across the cobbles and over the grass towards Millie, Lily and Newt who were already waiting for him at the theatre door.

Now he stared at the envelope in his hand. He'd not had the courage to open it earlier. He'd said he was late as an excuse, they would have waited for him, and he knew that, he'd just not had enough pluck to open it, and although the busy active's had distracted him, the letter had constantly bothered him, and he could no longer restrain his curiosity. He held the envelope to the cast of the lantern and slid his fingers over the writing. His Ma was right. It was the same style and type of army paper, but the handwriting was a different style to James's. Rain began to smudge the ink, and so he flipped it over and began to tear at the seal.

A growling rahhhh followed by a long purr at the road end near to the village distracted him and he raised his head to look beyond the group who, now halfway across the field to the theatre had also stopped and turned to look at the disturbance behind them.

"By God." Bertie mouthed. "She's come." Rapidly he stashed the letter into his rear pocket and, suddenly finding the need to look his best, he flattened his wet and wind-blown hair with his hand.

He never dreamt she would actually come. He wrote to her agent who had publicized his details under the promotion of 'Hadley Holmes's Travelling Vaudeville', but as immediately after posting the invitation, he abandoned all thoughts of unimaginable request.

He never thought she would ever receive his letter explaining the gang's dream to raise funds for the soldiers or break from her busy schedule to attend or even perform in the amateurs show.

He watched a Homberg wearing man in a long overcoat get out of the car, and look around as if he was surveying the area, then walk to the rear of the car to lift a travel case from the boot. Pausing again to swivel his head in all directions, the man then raised an umbrella and opened the passenger door.

'It's really her. Laney Dove.' His jaw hung loose, and his heart beat so fast he felt the need to rub his chest. He couldn't see the women's face. Her head was entirely covered with a large dark sou'wester, and she had quickly vanished from almost complete view under the large umbrella.

'I must tell Millie.' He didn't need to. As he turned to sprint towards the theatre door, he slammed straight into her.

Bertie couldn't help smiling as he fixed his hands on her shoulders to prevent her from falling backwards into the mud. "I'm sorry I didn't tell you." He firmed his grip excitedly. "But I never thought she'd come."

Bewildered, Millie gawked over Bertie's shoulder and across the field at a man who was struggling to hold the umbrella against the gusts. She narrowed her eyes on the almost concealed women as she was dragging passed Newt's Pa and his ogling companions.

"Bertie?" She frowned and wiped the rain from her forehead with the back of her hand. She inquisitively narrowed her eyes as she waited for him to explain.

"It's Laney Dove, and she's come to sing for us." He enthusiastically boasted.

She slanted her head and her neck seemed to stretch as she tried to improve her view.

"Sing?" She uttered with almost dumbfounded reticence.

"I haven't got time to explain, but."

"Are you the God darn nuisance that sent that awful letter?" Fiercely shouting as the couple rapidly approached Laney Dove's chaperone, cut Bertie off in mid-sentence.

"Err …… Yes Sir." He spun from Millie and stretched out his greeting hand. "Bertie Lanyon."

"Idiot." Grouched the man, ignoring the welcoming palm.

"Wallace, stop it." Laney shook off his linking and detaining arm. "We've been over this too many times already." She openly condemned his obvious disapproval. "So just stop it. Right now." Her enamel white face befit the stormy weather. "I don't' want to hear another word."

Angling her face towards Bertie, but remaining under the protection of the umbrella, a smile displaced her rage.

"Bertie, I'm Laney Dove." She reached out and delicately took his waiting hand to accept the welcome Wallace had dismissed.

178

"What a delightful idea. Thank you for inviting me." With the handshake, she gently tilted her face to glance and smile at Millie. "I'm delighted to be here, and to help in any way I can."

She released his cold hand and quickly retracted her arm under her bell sleeve. "Now can you please get me out of this dreadful weather and show me to my changing room."

Millie and Bertie looked at each other, their eyes displaying panic knowing all they could provide was the old bed sheet hung from pegs.

"Millie." Bertie tore his gaze away from the enticing artist and bluffed a smile. "Can you please lead the way?"

Millie feigned a smile. "Be my pleasure." And she spun, but hidden by the darkness, she kicked hard on Bertie's shin. "Please follow me."

Bumping deliberately into Bertie as he walked by him, Wallace's glare openly exposed his irritation and resentment of having to drive in terrible conditions for such an unrewarding cause. Noting the scowl, Laney Dove thrust her elbow into Wallace's midriff hard enough for him to exhale and not caring if anyone had noticed, she smiled and delicately nodded at the crowd who had now caught them up from the rear before requesting Millie to. "Lead the way, my dear girl."

"Thank you for doing this Bertie."

The praise and gratitude continued as the last spectators walked on behind the famed entertainer, some of them even patting Bertie on the shoulder, but instead of following them and entering the theatre, Bertie stood and gazed across the gloom towards South Cliff.

He shook his head and sighed glumly, knowing his Ma had not left her fireside chair. Then finally, after listening to the furor which seeped between the gaps in the lumber and the wind rattling door, he tapped on his back pocket and walked towards the theatre.

However, he did not swing back the door, and enter the theatre to join his friends, instead he strolled morosely straight passed the joviality, and walked to the blustery cliff top where after glancing over his shoulder to make sure no one had followed him he slumped to his knees, and looked up to the angry windswept clouds.

With the cold breath of winter howling across the noisy water, he pulled his jumper high around his neck and waited for the moon to emerge from the clouds.

29th September

To whom it may concern.

I am writing to you today to inform you of the terrible news that your Labrador retriever 'Finn' died today whist serving in active duty.

"No!" Echoing across the cliff tops, he repeated the scream from deep within his tormented soul.

 "Why?"

This new pain caused him to tremble, and tears united with the rain to deluge down his cheeks.

"No, God! No!"

Suddenly the salty air tasted foul and he retched and splattered his shoes with bile. Anger intertwined with pain and sadness clamped around his heart and forced him to pant for breath. Memories flooded back and he screamed. From within he raged and he unleashed a spirit previously unknown to him, an all-consuming demon of hate.

"I should have tried harder. I should have acted sooner. I should have been wiser."

Finn gave him everything, his love, his trust and his heart and in return, he had failed him. He couldn't breath, and gasping throat burning air he cursed God, his Ma, and the damned war. His heart was empty, now desolate of everything.

"I should not have trusted anyone. I should have run away and taken Finn with me."

He clamped tight his eyes and covered his ears with his hands to block out the distant sounds of joviality when a gust of wind tore the letter from his grasp to swirl and flutter it high into the pitch. He didn't care. Suddenly he'd recalled the warmth of Finn's breath, the softness of his fur, and the gladness he felt by seeing his happy tail wag when he returned home.

However, his love once more quickly turned to hate, and the hate brought more pain. He cussed again at the British army, the Germans and Drake. He staggered on the edge of the cliff enveloped in darkness as the storm raged above his head. Thunder crashes overhead, mirroring the turmoil within his mind.

His thoughts were a swirl of despair and hopelessness, whispering to him of a release that now only death could bring.

The howling wind beckoned him closer to the cliff edge and urged him to take that final step into oblivion.

Lightning flashed in the sky, illuminating his twisted and agonized face as he battled against the overwhelming urge to surrender to the dark impulse and leap into the beckoning waves that crashed against the rocks below. He couldn't hear them, but he knew they were there and he couldn't hear Millie calling out his name as she ran frantically and screamed in the darkness behind him. Despair had silenced everything.

He staggered uncontrollably on the edge of the cliff and stared out one last time into the dark abyss. From the loss and betrayal there was now a strange coldness within him, a chill disillusioned him and he was repulsively weary of life itself. *'They won't have buried him like they do the men…….. poor Finn. He will have been abandoned and discarded to just decay and sink into the mud.'* He couldn't endure anymore pain, without Finn all hope was lost and a consuming paranoia filled him with a sense of failure, regret and self-incrimination. With Finn gone, he had lost everything.

"Bertie! Bertie! Where are you?" Millie was certain she had seen him walking on the cliff top, but now all she could she was darkness, the occasional splash of moonlight, and blinding flashes in the distance. She shouted his name again. There was no reply, just a rumble of thunder and so she stared once more above the cliff tops, suspecting the storm had guiled her imagination. Cussing him for leaving her with the actress, she began to turn back towards the Alderthay, but as she did so a piece of paper blowing in the wind fluttered by her face. Without thought or reason, she instinctively grabbed the sodden paper and angled it to the moonlight.

182

29th September

To whom it may concern.

I am writing to you today to inform you of the terrible news that your Labrador retriever 'Finn' died today whist serving in active service.

She dropped to her knees and her world around her blackened in a discord of rain and despair, each droplet aggravating the anguish that poured from her heart. Thunder roared as she screamed, echoing her pain and suffocating her wails in nature's relentless barrage.

Feeling isolated and worthless in the tempest that raged both within and about, her fragile calls for help were crushed as the storm cruelly swallowed her plea's to leave her alone and shrouded in the darkness to struggle with her dreams crushed and abandoned. She cried into her hands as the wild gusts swirled around her like an evil taunting whisper that took away her breath and filled her heart with pain and dread.

'Finn? .... Bertie. No God. Please no. Not my Bertie.'

Other novels by Daniel Carlson include;

The Highwayman and the Spy

The Vengeance Trail

The Return

Life Taker - The Story of the Gun

A Kiss for the Cursed

The Apostle

The Life and Death of My Best Friend, Davy Crockett

The Betrayal

www.ingramcontent.com/pod-product-compliance
Ingram Content Group UK Ltd.
Pitfield, Milton Keynes, MK11 3LW, UK
UKHW010935220725
7011UKWH00030BA/177